CHILDREN'S CLASSICS
EVERYMAN'S LIBRARY

The Everyman
Book of
Nonsense Verse

Edited and introduced by
Louise Guinness

EVERYMAN'S LIBRARY
CHILDREN'S CLASSICS
Alfred A. Knopf New York London Toronto

THIS IS A BORZOI BOOK
PUBLISHED BY ALFRED A. KNOPF

First included in Everyman's Library Children's Classics, 2004
Design and typography Copyright © 2004 by Everyman's Library
Series design by Barbara de Wilde and Carol Devine Carson
This book typeset and designed by Yvonne Worth

A list of acknowledgements to copyright holders
appears at the back of this volume.

Five of Ernest H. Shepard's illustrations from *Dream Days*
by Kenneth Grahame are reprinted on the endpapers by
permission of The Bodley Head, London.
The sixth illustration is by S.C. Hulme Beaman.

Published in the United Kingdom by Everyman's Library,
Northburgh House, 10 Northburgh Street, London EC1V 0AT,
and distributed by Random House (UK) Ltd.

www.randomhouse.com/everymans (US)
www.randomhouse.co.uk (UK)

1-4000-4425-1 (US)

1-85715-514-9 (UK)

A CIP catalogue record for this book is available from the British Library

Printed and bound in Germany by GGP Media GmbH, Pössneck

CONTENTS

Contents

Contents

Contents

Contents

PREFACE

This selection has no pretensions towards being comprehensive. It has been the editor's task to present readers with samples of the work of the great nonsense writers and in some cases it has been necessary to limit one renowned author's contributions to fit in some so far lesser-known verses by another.

I have included all the verses that I used to recite when I was a child to amuse my brothers on long car journeys, and I therefore make no apology for presenting so many of Spike Milligan's verses, or for pillaging freely from my favourite anthologies such as *Oh How Silly!*

It is always difficult to decide what must be left out. The editor trusts that the reader will take pleasure in being scandalised by the oversights as well as being amused by the ridiculous nonsense included in this book.

INTRODUCTION

There is something intrinsically nonsensical about any attempt to explain nonsense verse. It speaks eloquently enough for itself but is difficult to define. Neither malicious enough for satire, nor derivative enough for parody, it also lacks that roistering quality associated with much comic verse. Nonsense is one of literature's oddities; it defies anyone to take it seriously, but has an endearing unruly charm. Nonsense has a misfit status; it is a rebellious and anarchic invention, its authors having resisted the most basic of all restraints on a writer: that of the obligation to make sense. Lewis Carroll's matchless exploration of the subject of nonsense comes in the form of *Alice's Adventures in Wonderland* and *Through the Looking-Glass*. Poor Alice – she fights so bravely in the cause of Reason, but the battalions of preposterous characters conspiring to bewilder her with ideas from the edge of lunacy inevitably wear her down. When the White Rabbit reads out some verses during the trial of the hapless Knave of Hearts, Alice offers to give anyone sixpence if they can explain them: 'I', she declares, 'don't believe there's an atom of meaning in it.' The King of Hearts has the answer to this: 'If there's no meaning in it … that saves a world of trouble, you know, as we needn't try to find any. And yet I don't know', he continues thoughtfully, '…I seem to see some meaning in them after all.' This is the essence of all the greatest nonsense, in both poetry and prose: however inappropriate the situation, however extravagant, absurd and, above all, unlikely the scenes described, we seem 'to see some meaning in them after all'. The meaning we find comes from somewhere other than the usual logical collection of phrases and words: it comes from the writers' extraordinary ability to bestow upon the most outlandish creatures and situations a poignant scrap of humanity that we recognise.

It is the peculiar genius of the writer of successful nonsense to be able to tell a story, conjure up a vivid image or evoke an atmosphere using the rhythm, the cadence and the sound of words – some of which may never have made any previous appearance in any known language. 'Jabberwocky', for example, can be read and understood by quite small children who will readily grasp the menacing quality of the Jabberwock with eyes of flame, whiffling through the tulgey wood.

The appeal of nonsense verse might be partly to do with early memories of those jumbled words of nursery rhymes, but while sharing the simple rhythmic qualities of the likes of 'Goosey, Goosey Gander' the best examples have a much harder edge. Nonsense poetry can be both very sad and ruthlessly cruel. Think of the oysters in 'The Walrus and the Carpenter' whose fate is sealed in spite of the walrus's momentary prick of conscience: ' "It seems a shame," the walrus said, "To play them such a trick,/After we've brought them out so far,/And made them trot so quick!" ' The macabre nature of the scene is emphasised by the camaraderie of the Walrus and the Carpenter with their victims. They seem fond of the little bivalves and it is with a growing sense of horror that we become aware of their true intentions. The last verse of the poem reminds us of this contradiction and the final line is chillingly heartless:

'O Oysters,' said the Carpenter,
   'You've had a pleasant run!
Shall we be trotting home again?'
   But answer came there none –
And this was scarcely odd, because
   They'd eaten every one.

There is a distinctly melancholic quality to another of the most famous nonsense poems, 'The Owl and the Pussy-cat' by Edward Lear. This is a love story between two of the most ill-suited characters since Titania fell for Bottom. They are wonderfully mismatched – think how much of the poignancy would be lost if an owl and an owl had gone to sea. When they sail away for a year and a day their journey seems to reflect the yearning of all lovers to be alone together, free from the interference and the distraction of a disapproving world. Once they have set sail, the sweetness of their courtship is helped along by encounters with other strange beings: they go to a land where the bong tree grows; they find a pig who's willing to do a spot of trading; they're married by a turkey and they eat their wedding feast with a runcible spoon. The image of the Owl and the Pussy-cat dancing by the light of the moon transcends its own peculiarity through the haunting lyricism which catches at the heart:

And hand in hand, on the edge of the sand,
   They danced by the light of the moon,
     The moon,
     The moon,
   They danced by the light of the moon.

Introduction

The Owl and the Pussy-cat are typical of the characters that generally inhabit the world of nonsense. So very often they are outsiders and misfits with impossible desires and improbable physical attributes which make them different. The Pobble, we are told, once had as many toes as we, but that was then...; how Spike Milligan's 'Hipporhinostricow' came to be we'll never know; Edward Gorey's confused beings are almost luminous in their eerie oddness, but they're signalling wildly to be understood; Quentin Blake's 'Mr Magnolia' may have two lovely sisters who play on the flute, but he can't be part of the mainstream because he has only one boot; and as for 'The Akond of Swat', someone might know who or which or why or what is the Akond of Swat, but I doubt it. The truly exotic Akond of Swat will always be wreathed in a kind of enigmatic mist.

It is no accident that nonsense verse really took hold of the public imagination in the Victorian era. A time of such unparalleled earnestness was bound to have a backlash and it came in the form of a delight in absurdity that in the context of the times would have had the added appeal of being shocking. The genius of Edward Lear and of Lewis Carroll was their ability to introduce the subversive notion of fun and delight in a form that challenged the moral seriousness of the age. The lofty tone of some of this verse is ludicrously at odds with the content and it is this gap between style and content that so often makes us laugh. The Victorian certainties about the importance of fact, purity and respectability are questioned by the topsy-turvy world of nonsense. The mildly outraged tone of Gelett Burgess's 'Purple Cow' hilariously parodies the lofty determination of one who resolves to be steadfast in the face of anything unusual. The poem's protagonist has the air of one who knows his own mind and has solemnly and rather stoically prepared himself for every eventuality, including that of seeing, or even being, a purple cow.

Inflated egos and pomposity are undermined by sheer absurdity and often by very enjoyable silliness; by the daring message that there might be some point in writing for simple delight, for the exuberant and playful fun of it all. A love of nonsense is best nurtured in early childhood but nonsense can be appreciated at any age. It is to take pleasure in the elasticity and potential of our language and the fascination with the possibility of other worlds. The King of Hearts was right: there may be little common sense in these verses but there is indeed some uncommon meaning in them after all.

To my darling children
Molly, Hector, Arthur, Matthew and Sam.

The Everyman
Book of
Nonsense Verse

Anonymous

DICKERY, DICKERY, DARE

Dickery, dickery, dare,
The pig flew up in the air;
The man in brown
Soon brought him down,
Dickery, dickery, dare.

Hilaire Belloc

THE FROG

Be kind and tender to the Frog,
　　And do not call him names,
As 'Slimy skin', or 'Polly-wog',
　　Or likewise 'Ugly James',
Or 'Gape-a-grin', or 'Toad-gone-wrong',
　　Or 'Billy Bandy-knees':
The Frog is justly sensitive
　　To epithets like these.
No animal will more repay
　　A treatment kind and fair;
At least so lonely people say
Who keep a frog (and, by the way,
　　They are extremely rare).

Anonymous

BE LENIENT WITH LOBSTERS

Be lenient with lobsters, and even kind to crabs,
And be not disrespectful to cuttlefish or dabs;
Chase not the Cochin-China, chaff not the ox obese,
And babble not of feather-beds in company with geese.
Be tender with the tadpole, and let the limpet thrive,
Be merciful to mussels, don't skin your eels alive;
When talking to a turtle don't mention calipee –
Be always kind to animals wherever you may be.

THE MAN-MOTH★

Here, above,
cracks in the buildings are filled with battered moonlight.
The whole shadow of Man is only as big as his hat.
It lies at his feet like a circle for a doll to stand on,
and he makes an inverted pin, the point magnetized to the moon.
He does not see the moon; he observes only her vast properties,
feeling the queer light on his hands, neither warm nor cold,
of a temperature impossible to record in thermometers.

But when the Man-Moth
pays his rare, although occasional, visits to the surface,
the moon looks rather different to him. He emerges
from an opening under the edge of one of the sidewalks
and nervously begins to scale the faces of the buildings.
He thinks the moon is a small hole at the top of the sky,
proving the sky quite useless for protection.
He trembles, but must investigate as high as he can climb.

Up the façades,
his shadow dragging like a photographer's cloth behind him,
he climbs fearfully, thinking that this time he will manage
to push his small head through that round clean opening
and be forced through, as from a tube, in black scrolls on the light.
(Man, standing below him, has no such illusions.)
But what the Man-Moth fears most he must do, although
he fails, of course, and falls back scared but quite unhurt.

    Then he returns
to the pale subways of cement he calls his home. He flits,
he flutters, and cannot get aboard the silent trains
fast enough to suit him. The doors close swiftly.
The Man-Moth always seats himself facing the wrong way
and the train starts at once at its full, terrible speed,
without a shift in gears or a gradation of any sort.
He cannot tell the rate at which he travels backwards.

    Each night he must
be carried through artificial tunnels and dream recurrent dreams.
Just as the ties recur beneath his train, these underlie
his rushing brain. He does not dare look out the window,
for the third rail, the unbroken draught of poison,
runs there beside him. He regards it as a disease
he has inherited the susceptibility to. He has to keep
his hands in his pockets, as others must wear mufflers.

    If you catch him,
hold up a flashlight to his eye. It's all dark pupil,
an entire night itself, whose haired horizon tightens
as he stares back, and closes up the eye. Then from the lids
one tear, his only possession, like the bee's sting, slips.
Slyly he palms it, and if you're not paying attention
he'll swallow it. However, if you watch, he'll hand it over,
cool as from underground springs and pure enough to drink.

★Newspaper misprint for 'mammoth'.

MR MAGNOLIA

Mr Magnolia has only one boot.

Quentin Blake

He has an old trumpet
that goes rooty-toot –

And two lovely sisters
who play on the flute –

But Mr Magnolia has only one boot.

Quentin Blake

In his pond live a frog
    and a toad and a newt –

32

33

Quentin Blake

He has green parakeets
   who pick holes in his suit –

35

Quentin Blake

And some very fat owls
    who are learning to hoot –
But Mr Magnolia
    has only one boot.

Gelett Burgess

PURPLE COW

I never saw a Purple Cow,
    I never hope to see one,
But I can tell you, anyhow,
    I'd rather see than be one!

JABBERWOCKY

'Twas brillig, and the slithy toves
    Did gyre and gimble in the wabe;
All mimsy were the borogoves,
    And the mome raths outgrabe.

'Beware the Jabberwock, my son!
    The jaws that bite, the claws that catch!
Beware the Jubjub bird, and shun
    The frumious Bandersnatch!'

He took his vorpal sword in hand:
    Long time the manxome foe he sought –
So rested he by the Tumtum tree,
    And stood awhile in thought.

And as in uffish thought he stood,
    The Jabberwock, with eyes of flame,
Came whiffling through the tulgey wood,
    And burbled as it came!

One, two! One, two! And through and through
    The vorpal blade went snicker-snack!
He left it dead, and with its head
    He went galumphing back.

'And hast thou slain the Jabberwock?
　　Come to my arms, my beamish boy!
O frabjous day! Callooh! Callay!'
　　He chortled in his joy.

'Twas brillig, and the slithy toves
　　Did gyre and gimble in the wabe;
All mimsy were the borogoves,
　　And the mome raths outgrabe.

Lewis Carroll

TWINKLE, TWINKLE, LITTLE BAT!

Twinkle, twinkle, little bat!
How I wonder what you're at!
Up above the world you fly,
Like a tea-tray in the sky.
    Twinkle, twinkle —

THE MOCK TURTLE'S SONG

'Will you walk a little faster?' said a whiting to a snail,
'There's a porpoise close behind us, and he's treading
    on my tail.
See how eagerly the lobsters and the turtles all advance!
They are waiting on the shingle – will you come and
    join the dance?
Will you, won't you, will you, won't you, will you join the
    dance?
Will you, won't you, will you, won't you, won't you join the
    dance?

'You can really have no notion how delightful it will be
When they take us up and throw us, with the lobsters,
    out to sea!'
But the snail replied, 'Too far, too far!' and gave a look askance –
Said he thanked the whiting kindly, but he would not join the
    dance.
Would not, could not, would not, could not, would not join the
    dance.
Would not, could not, would not, could not, could not join the
    dance.

'What matters it how far we go?' his scaly friend replied,
"There is another shore, you know, upon the other side.
The further off from England the nearer is to France –
Then turn not pale, beloved snail, but come and join the dance.
Will you, won't you, will you, won't you, will you join the
    dance?
Will you, won't you, will you, won't you, won't you join the
    dance?'

Lewis Carroll

THE CROCODILE

How doth the little crocodile
    Improve his shining tail,
And pour the waters of the Nile
    On every golden scale!

How cheerfully he seems to grin!
    How neatly spread his claws,
And welcomes little fishes in
    With gently smiling jaws!

Lewis Carroll

THE GARDENER'S SONG

He thought he saw an Elephant,
    That practised on a fife:
He looked again, and found it was
    A letter from his wife.
'At length I realise,' he said,
    'The bitterness of Life!'

He thought he saw a Buffalo
    Upon the chimney-piece:
He looked again, and found it was
    His Sister's Husband's Niece.
'Unless you leave this house,' he said,
    'I'll send for the Police!'

He thought he saw a Rattlesnake
    That questioned him in Greek:
He looked again, and found it was
    The Middle of Next Week.
'The one thing I regret,' he said,
    'Is that it cannot speak!'

He thought he saw a Banker's Clerk
    Descending from the bus:
He looked again, and found it was
    A Hippopotamus
'If this should stay to dine,' he said,
    'There won't be much for us!'

He thought he saw a Kangaroo
    That worked a coffee-mill:
He looked again, and found it was
    A Vegetable-Pill.
'Were I to swallow this,' he said,
    'I should be very ill!'

He thought he saw a Coach-and-Four
    That stood beside his bed:
He looked again, and found it was
    A Bear without a Head.
'Poor thing,' he said, 'poor silly thing!
    It's waiting to be fed!'

He thought he saw an Albatross
    That fluttered round the lamp:
He looked again, and found it was
    A Penny-Postage-Stamp.
'You'd best be getting home,' he said:
    'The nights are very damp!'

He thought he saw a Garden-Door
    That opened with a key:
He looked again, and found it was
    A double Rule of Three:
'And all its mystery,' he said,
    'Is clear as day to me!'

He thought he saw an Argument
    That proved he was the Pope
He looked again, and found it was
    A Bar of Mottled Soap.
'A fact so dread,' he faintly said,
    'Extinguishes all hope!'

Lewis Carroll

THE HUNTING OF THE SNARK

Lewis Carroll

Fit the First – THE LANDING

'Just the place for a Snark!' the Bellman cried,
As he landed his crew with care;
Supporting each man on the top of the tide
By a finger entwined in his hair.

'Just the place for a Snark! I have said it twice:
That alone should encourage the crew.
Just the place for a Snark! I have said it thrice:
What I tell you three times is true.'

The crew was complete: it included a Boots –
A maker of Bonnets and Hoods –
A Barrister, brought to arrange their disputes –
And a Broker, to value their goods.

A Billiard-marker, whose skill was immense,
Might perhaps have won more than his share –
But a Banker, engaged at enormous expense,
Had the whole of their cash in his care.

There was also a Beaver, that paced on the deck,
Or would sit making lace in the bow:
And had often (the Bellman said) saved them from wreck,
Though none of the sailors knew how.

There was one who was famed for the number of things
He forgot when he entered the ship:
His umbrella, his watch, all his jewels and rings,
And the clothes he had bought for the trip.

He had forty-two boxes, all carefully packed,
With his name painted clearly on each:
But, since he omitted to mention the fact,
They were all left behind on the beach.

The loss of his clothes hardly mattered, because
He had seven coats on when he came,
With three pairs of boots – but the worst of it was,
He had wholly forgotten his name.

He would answer to 'Hi!' or to any loud cry,
Such as 'Fry me!' or 'Fritter my wig!'
To 'What-you-may-call-um!' or 'What-was-his-name!'
But especially 'Thing-um-a-jig!'

While, for those who preferred a more forcible word,
He had different names from these:
His intimate friends called him 'Candle-ends',
And his enemies 'Toasted-cheese'.

'His form is ungainly – his intellect small – '
(So the Bellman would often remark)
'But his courage is perfect! And that, after all,
Is the thing that one needs with a Snark.'

He would joke with hyenas, returning their stare
With an impudent wag of the head:
And he once went a walk, paw-in-paw, with a bear,
'Just to keep up its spirits,' he said.

He came as a Baker: but owned when too late –
And it drove the poor Bellman half-mad –
He could only bake Bridecake – for which, I may state,
No materials were to be had.

The last of the crew needs especial remark,
Though he looked an incredible dunce:
He had just one idea – but, that one being 'Snark',
The good Bellman engaged him at once.

He came as a Butcher: but gravely declared,
When the ship had been sailing a week,
He could only kill Beavers. The Bellman looked scared,
And was almost too frightened to speak:

But at length he explained, in a tremulous tone,
There was only one Beaver on board;
And that was a tame one he had of his own,
Whose death would be deeply deplored.

The Beaver, who happened to hear the remark,
Protested, with tears in its eyes,
That not even the rapture of hunting the Snark
Could atone for that dismal surprise!

It strongly advised that the Butcher should be
Conveyed in a separate ship:
But the Bellman declared that would never agree
With the plans he had made for the trip:

Navigation was always a difficult art,
Though with only one ship and one bell:
And he feared he must really decline, for his part,
Undertaking another as well.

The Beaver's best course was, no doubt, to procure
A second-hand dagger-proof coat –
So the Baker advised it—and next, to insure
Its life in some Office of note:

This the Baker suggested, and offered for hire
(On moderate terms), or for sale,
Two excellent Policies, one Against Fire,
And one Against Damage From Hail.

Yet still, ever after that sorrowful day,
Whenever the Butcher was by,
The Beaver kept looking the opposite way,
And appeared unaccountably shy.

FIT THE SECOND - THE BELLMAN'S SPEECH

The Bellman himself they all praised to the skies –
Such a carriage, such ease and such grace!
Such solemnity, too! One could see he was wise,
The moment one looked in his face!

He had bought a large map representing the sea,
Without the least vestige of land:
And the crew were much pleased when they found it to be
A map they could all understand.

'What's the good of Mercator's North Poles and Equators,
Tropics, Zones, and Meridian Lines?'
So the Bellman would cry: and the crew would reply
'They are merely conventional signs!

'Other maps are such shapes, with their islands and capes!
But we've got our brave Captain to thank'
(So the crew would protest) 'that he's bought us the best –
A perfect and absolute blank!'

This was charming, no doubt; but they shortly found out
That the Captain they trusted so well
Had only one notion for crossing the ocean,
And that was to tingle his bell.

Lewis Carroll

He was thoughtful and grave – but the orders he gave
Were enough to bewilder a crew.
When he cried 'Steer to starboard, but keep her head larboard!'
What on earth was the helmsman to do?

Then the bowsprit got mixed with the rudder sometimes:
A thing, as the Bellman remarked,
That frequently happens in tropical climes,
When a vessel is, so to speak, 'snarked'.

But the principal failing occurred in the sailing,
And the Bellman, perplexed and distressed,
Said he *had* hoped, at least, when the wind blew due East,
That the ship would *not* travel due West!

But the danger was past – they had landed at last,
With their boxes, portmanteaus, and bags:
Yet at first sight the crew were not pleased with the view,
Which consisted of chasms and crags.

The Bellman perceived that their spirits were low,
And repeated in musical tone
Some jokes he had kept for a season of woe –
But the crew would do nothing but groan.

He served out some grog with a liberal hand,
And bade them sit down on the beach:
And they could not but own that their Captain looked grand,
As he stood and delivered his speech.

'Friends, Romans, and countrymen, lend me your ears!'
(They were all of them fond of quotations:
So they drank to his health, and they gave him three cheers,
While he served out additional rations.)

'We have sailed many months, we have sailed many weeks,
(Four weeks to the month you may mark),
But never as yet ('tis your Captain who speaks)
Have we caught the least glimpse of a Snark!

'We have sailed many weeks, we have sailed many days,
(Seven days to the week I allow),
But a Snark, on the which we might lovingly gaze,
We have never beheld till now!

'Come, listen, my men, while I tell you again
The five unmistakable marks
By which you may know, wheresoever you go,
The warranted genuine Snarks.

'Let us take them in order. The first is the taste,
Which is meagre and hollow, but crisp:
Like a coat that is rather too tight in the waist,
With a flavour of Will-o'-the-wisp.

'Its habit of getting up late you'll agree
That it carries too far, when I say
That it frequently breakfasts at five-o'clock tea,
And dines on the following day.

'The third is its slowness in taking a jest.
Should you happen to venture on one,
It will sigh like a thing that is deeply distressed:
And it always looks grave at a pun.

'The fourth is its fondness for bathing-machines,
Which it constantly carries about,
And believes that they add to the beauty of scenes –
A sentiment open to doubt.

'The fifth is ambition. It next will be right
To describe each particular batch:
Distinguishing those that have feathers, and bite,
And those that have whiskers, and scratch.

Lewis Carroll

'For, although common Snarks do no manner of harm,
Yet, I feel it my duty to say,
Some are Boojums –' The Bellman broke off in alarm,
For the Baker had fainted away.

FIT THE THIRD - THE BAKER'S TALE

They roused him with muffins – they roused him with ice –
They roused him with mustard and cress –
They roused him with jam and judicious advice –
They set him conundrums to guess.

When at length he sat up and was able to speak,
His sad story he offered to tell;
And the Bellman cried 'Silence! not even a shriek!'
And excitedly tingled his bell.

There was silence supreme! Not a shriek, not a scream,
Scarcely even a howl or a groan,
As the man they called 'Ho!' told his story of woe
In an antediluvian tone.

'My father and mother were honest, though poor –'
'Skip all that!' cried the Bellman in haste.
'If it once becomes dark, there's no chance of a Snark –
We have hardly a minute to waste!'

'I skip forty years,' said the Baker, in tears,
'And proceed without further remark
To the day when you took me aboard of your ship
To help you in hunting the Snark.

'A dear uncle of mine (after whom I was named)
Remarked, when I bade him farewell –'
'Oh, skip your dear uncle!' the Bellman exclaimed,
As he angrily tingled his bell.

'He remarked to me then,' said that mildest of men,
'"If your Snark be a Snark, that is right:
Fetch it home by all means – you may serve it with greens,
And it's handy for striking a light.

'"You may seek it with thimbles – and seek it with care;
You may hunt it with forks and hope;
You may threaten its life with a railway-share;
You may charm it with smiles and soap –"'

('That's exactly the method,' the Bellman bold
In a hasty parenthesis cried,
'That's exactly the way I have always been told
That the capture of Snarks should be tried!')

'"But oh, beamish nephew, beware of the day,
If your Snark be a Boojum! For then
You will softly and suddenly vanish away,
And never be met with again!"

'It is this, it is this that oppresses my soul,
When I think of my uncle's last words:
And my heart is like nothing so much as a bowl
Brimming over with quivering curds!

'It is this, it is this –' 'We have had that before!'
The Bellman indignantly said.
And the Baker replied 'Let me say it once more.
It is this, it is this that I dread!

'I engage with the Snark — every night after dark —
In a dreamy delirious fight:
I serve it with greens in those shadowy scenes,
And I use it for striking a light:

'But if ever I meet with a Boojum, that day,
In a moment (of this I am sure),
I shall softly and suddenly vanish away —
And the notion I cannot endure!'

Lewis Carroll

Fit the Fourth – THE HUNTING

The Bellman looked uffish, and wrinkled his brow.
'If only you'd spoken before!
It's excessively awkward to mention it now,
With the Snark, so to speak, at the door!

'We should all of us grieve, as you well may believe,
If you never were met with again –
But surely, my man, when the voyage began,
You might have suggested it then?

'It's excessively awkward to mention it now –
As I think I've already remarked.'
And the man they called 'Hi!' replied, with a sigh,
'I informed you the day we embarked.

'You may charge me with murder – or want of sense –
(We are all of us weak at times):
But the slightest approach to a false pretence
Was never among my crimes!

'I said it in Hebrew – I said it in Dutch –
I said it in German and Greek;
But I wholly forgot (and it vexes me much)
That English is what you speak!'

Lewis Carroll

''Tis a pitiful tale,' said the Bellman, whose face
Had grown longer at every word:
'But, now that you've stated the whole of your case,
More debate would be simply absurd.

'The rest of my speech' (he explained to his men)
'You shall hear when I've leisure to speak it.
But the Snark is at hand, let me tell you again!
'Tis your glorious duty to seek it!

'To seek it with thimbles, to seek it with care;
To pursue it with forks and hope;
To threaten its life with a railway-share;
To charm it with smiles and soap!

'For the Snark's a peculiar creature, that won't
Be caught in a commonplace way.
Do all that you know, and try all that you don't:
Not a chance must be wasted to-day!

'For England expects – I forbear to proceed:
'Tis a maxim tremendous, but trite:
And you'd best be unpacking the things that you need
To rig yourselves out for the fight.'

Then the Banker endorsed a blank cheque (which he crossed),
And changed his loose silver for notes.
The Baker with care combed his whiskers and hair,
And shook the dust out of his coats.

The Boots and the Broker were sharpening a spade –
Each working the grindstone in turn;
But the Beaver went on making lace, and displayed
No interest in the concern:

Though the Barrister tried to appeal to its pride,
And vainly proceeded to cite
A number of cases, in which making laces
Had been proved an infringement of right.

The maker of Bonnets ferociously planned
A novel arrangement of bows:
While the Billiard-marker with quivering hand
Was chalking the tip of his nose.

But the Butcher turned nervous, and dressed himself fine,
With yellow kid gloves and a ruff –
Said he felt it exactly like going to dine,
Which the Bellman declared was all 'stuff'.

'Introduce me, now there's a good fellow,' he said,
'If we happen to meet it together!'
And the Bellman, sagaciously nodding his head,
Said 'That must depend on the weather.'

The Beaver went simply galumphing about,
At seeing the Butcher so shy:
And even the Baker, though stupid and stout,
Made an effort to wink with one eye.

'Be a man!' said the Bellman in wrath, as he heard
The Butcher beginning to sob.
'Should we meet with a Jubjub, that desperate bird,
We shall need all our strength for the job!'

Lewis Carroll

FIT THE FIFTH – THE BEAVER'S LESSON

They sought it with thimbles, they sought it with care;
They pursued it with forks and hope;
They threatened its life with a railway-share;
They charmed it with smiles and soap.

Then the Butcher contrived an ingenious plan
For making a separate sally;
And fixed on a spot unfrequented by man,
A dismal and desolate valley.

But the very same plan to the Beaver occurred:
It had chosen the very same place:
Yet neither betrayed, by a sign or a word,
The disgust that appeared in his face.

Each thought he was thinking of nothing but 'Snark'
And the glorious work of the day;
And each tried to pretend that he did not remark
That the other was going that way.

But the valley grew narrow and narrower still,
And the evening got darker and colder,
Till (merely from nervousness, not from goodwill)
They marched along shoulder to shoulder.

Lewis Carroll

Then a scream, shrill and high, rent the shuddering sky,
And they knew that some danger was near:
The Beaver turned pale to the tip of its tail,
And even the Butcher felt queer.

He thought of his childhood, left far far behind –
That blissful and innocent state –
The sound so exactly recalled to his mind
A pencil that squeaks on a slate!

''Tis the voice of the Jubjub!' he suddenly cried.
(This man, that they used to call 'Dunce'.)
'As the Bellman would tell you,' he added with pride,
'I have uttered that sentiment once.

''Tis the note of the Jubjub! Keep count, I entreat;
You will find I have told it you twice.
'Tis the song of the Jubjub! The proof is complete,
If only I've stated it thrice.'

The Beaver had counted with scrupulous care,
Attending to every word:
But it fairly lost heart, and outgrabe in despair,
When the third repetition occurred.

It felt that, in spite of all possible pains,
It had somehow contrived to lose count,
And the only thing now was to rack its poor brains
By reckoning up the amount.

'Two added to one – if that could but be done,'
It said, 'with one's fingers and thumbs!'
Recollecting with tears how, in earlier years,
It had taken no pains with its sums.

'The thing can be done,' said the Butcher, 'I think.
The thing must be done, I am sure.
The thing shall be done! Bring me paper and ink,
The best there is time to procure.'

The Beaver brought paper, portfolio, pens,
And ink in unfailing supplies:
While strange creepy creatures came out of their dens,
And watched them with wondering eyes.

So engrossed was the Butcher, he heeded them not,
As he wrote with a pen in each hand,
And explained all the while in a popular style
Which the Beaver could well understand.

'Taking Three as the subject to reason about –
A convenient number to state –
We add Seven, and Ten, and then multiply out
By One Thousand diminished by Eight.

'The result we proceed to divide, as you see,
By Nine Hundred and Ninety Two:
Then subtract Seventeen, and the answer must be
Exactly and perfectly true.

'The method employed I would gladly explain,
While I have it so clear in my head,
If I had but the time and you had but the brain –
But much yet remains to be said.

'In one moment I've seen what has hitherto been
Enveloped in absolute mystery,
And without extra charge I will give you at large
A Lesson in Natural History.'

In his genial way he proceeded to say
(Forgetting all laws of propriety,
And that giving instruction, without introduction,
Would have caused quite a thrill in Society),

'As to temper the Jubjub's a desperate bird,
Since it lives in perpetual passion:
Its taste in costume is entirely absurd –
It is ages ahead of the fashion:

'But it knows any friend it has met once before:
It never will look at a bribe:
And in charity-meetings it stands at the door,
And collects – though it does not subscribe.

'Its flavour when cooked is more exquisite far
Than mutton, or oysters, or eggs:
(Some think it keeps best in an ivory jar,
And some, in mahogany kegs:)

'You boil it in sawdust: you salt it in glue:
You condense it with locusts and tape:
Still keeping one principal object in view –
To preserve its symmetrical shape.'

The Butcher would gladly have talked till next day,
But he felt that the Lesson must end,
And he wept with delight in attempting to say
He considered the Beaver his friend.

While the Beaver confessed, with affectionate looks
More eloquent even than tears,
It had learnt in ten minutes far more than all books
Would have taught it in seventy years.

They returned hand-in-hand, and the Bellman, unmanned
(For a moment) with noble emotion,
Said 'This amply repays all the wearisome days
We have spent on the billowy ocean!'

Such friends, as the Beaver and Butcher became,
Have seldom if ever been known;
In winter or summer, 'twas always the same –
You could never meet either alone.

And when quarrels arose – as one frequently finds
Quarrels will, spite of every endeavour –
The song of the Jubjub recurred to their minds,
And cemented their friendship for ever!

Lewis Carroll

Fit the Sixth - THE BARRISTER'S DREAM

They sought it with thimbles, they sought it with care;
They pursued it with forks and hope;
They threatened its life with a railway-share;
They charmed it with smiles and soap.

But the Barrister, weary of proving in vain
That the Beaver's lace-making was wrong,
Fell asleep, and in dreams saw the creature quite plain
That his fancy had dwelt on so long.

He dreamed that he stood in a shadowy Court,
Where the Snark, with a glass in its eye,
Dressed in gown, bands, and wig, was defending a pig
On the charge of deserting its sty.

The Witnesses proved, without error or flaw,
That the sty was deserted when found:
And the Judge kept explaining the state of the law
In a soft under-current of sound.

The indictment had never been clearly expressed,
And it seemed that the Snark had begun,
And had spoken three hours, before any one guessed
What the pig was supposed to have done.

The Jury had each formed a different view
(Long before the indictment was read),
And they all spoke at once, so that none of them knew
One word that the others had said.

'You must know –' said the Judge: but the Snark exclaimed
   'Fudge!'
That statute is obsolete quite!
Let me tell you, my friends, the whole question depends
On an ancient manorial right.

'In the matter of Treason the pig would appear
To have aided, but scarcely abetted:
While the charge of Insolvency fails, it is clear,
If you grant the plea "never indebted".

'The fact of Desertion I will not dispute;
But its guilt, as I trust, is removed
(So far as relates to the costs of this suit)
By the Alibi which has been proved.

'My poor client's fate now depends on your votes.'
Here the speaker sat down in his place,
And directed the Judge to refer to his notes
And briefly to sum up the case.

But the Judge said he never had summed up before;
So the Snark undertook it instead,
And summed it so well that it came to far more
Than the Witnesses ever had said!

Lewis Carroll

When the verdict was called for, the Jury declined,
As the word was so puzzling to spell;
But they ventured to hope that the Snark wouldn't mind
Undertaking that duty as well.

So the Snark found the verdict, although, as it owned,
It was spent with the toils of the day:
When it said the word 'GUILTY!' the Jury all groaned,
And some of them fainted away.

Then the Snark pronounced sentence, the Judge being quite
Too nervous to utter a word:
When it rose to its feet, there was silence like night,
And the fall of a pin might be heard.

'Transportation for life' was the sentence it gave,
'And *then* to be fined forty pound.'
The Jury all cheered, though the Judge said he feared
That the phrase was not legally sound.

But their wild exultation was suddenly checked
When the jailer informed them, with tears,
Such a sentence would have not the slightest effect,
As the pig had been dead for some years.

Lewis Carroll

The Judge left the Court, looking deeply disgusted:
But the Snark, though a little aghast,
As the lawyer to whom the defence was intrusted,
Went bellowing on to the last.

Thus the Barrister dreamed, while the bellowing seemed
To grow every moment more clear:
Till he woke to the knell of a furious bell,
Which the Bellman rang close at his ear.

FIT THE SEVENTH - THE BANKER'S FATE

They sought it with thimbles, they sought it with care;
They pursued it with forks and hope;
They threatened its life with a railway-share;
They charmed it with smiles and soap.

And the Banker, inspired with a courage so new
It was matter for general remark,
Rushed madly ahead and was lost to their view
In his zeal to discover the Snark.

But while he was seeking with thimbles and care,
A Bandersnatch swiftly drew nigh
And grabbed at the Banker, who shrieked in despair,
For he knew it was useless to fly.

He offered large discount – he offered a cheque
(Drawn 'to bearer') for seven-pounds-ten:
But the Bandersnatch merely extended its neck
And grabbed at the Banker again.

Without rest or pause – while those frumious jaws
Went savagely snapping around –
He skipped and he hopped, and he floundered and flopped,
Till fainting he fell to the ground.

The Bandersnatch fled as the others appeared
Led on by that fear-stricken yell:
And the Bellman remarked 'It is just as I feared!'
And solemnly tolled on his bell.

He was black in the face, and they scarcely could trace
The least likeness to what he had been:
While so great was his fright that his waistcoat turned white –
A wonderful thing to be seen!

To the horror of all who were present that day.
He uprose in full evening dress,
And with senseless grimaces endeavoured to say
What his tongue could no longer express.

Down he sank in a chair – ran his hands through his hair –
And chanted in mimsiest tones
Words whose utter inanity proved his insanity,
While he rattled a couple of bones.

'Leave him here to his fate – it is getting so late!'
The Bellman exclaimed in a fright.
'We have lost half the day. Any further delay,
And we sha'n't catch a Snark before night!'

Lewis Carroll

FIT THE EIGHTH – THE VANISHING

They sought it with thimbles, they sought it with care;
They pursued it with forks and hope;
They threatened its life with a railway-share;
They charmed it with smiles and soap.

They shuddered to think that the chase might fail,
And the Beaver, excited at last,
Went bounding along on the tip of its tail,
For the daylight was nearly past.

'There is Thingumbob shouting!' the Bellman said,
'He is shouting like mad, only hark!
He is waving his hands, he is wagging his head,
He has certainly found a Snark!'

They gazed in delight, while the Butcher exclaimed
'He was always a desperate wag!'
They beheld him – their Baker – their hero unnamed –
On the top of a neighbouring crag.

Erect and sublime, for one moment of time.
In the next, that wild figure they saw
(As if stung by a spasm) plunge into a chasm,
While they waited and listened in awe.

'It's a Snark!' was the sound that first came to their ears,
And seemed almost too good to be true.
Then followed a torrent of laughter and cheers:
Then the ominous words 'It's a Boo —'

Then, silence. Some fancied they heard in the air
A weary and wandering sigh
That sounded like '–jum!' but the others declare
It was only a breeze that went by.

They hunted till darkness came on, but they found
Not a button, or feather, or mark,
By which they could tell that they stood on the ground
Where the Baker had met with the Snark.

In the midst of the word he was trying to say,
In the midst of his laughter and glee,
He had softly and suddenly vanished away —
For the Snark *was* a Boojum, you see.

THE END

THERE WAS A PIG

There was a Pig, that sat alone,
    Beside a ruined pump.
By day and night he made his moan:
It would have stirred a heart of stone
    To see him wring his hoofs and groan,
Because he could not jump.

Lewis Carroll

TWEEDLEDUM AND TWEEDLEDEE

Tweedledum and Tweedledee
    Agreed to have a battle;
For Tweedledum said Tweedledee
    Had spoiled his nice new rattle.

Just then flew down a monstrous crow,
    As black as a tar-barrel;
Which frightened both the heroes so,
    They quite forgot their quarrel.

BEAUTIFUL SOUP

Beautiful Soup, so rich and green,
Waiting in a hot tureen!
Who for such dainties would not stoop?
Soup of the evening, beautiful Soup!
Soup of the evening, beautiful Soup!
    Beau – ootiful Soo – oop!
    Beau – ootiful Soo – oop!
Soo – oop of the e – e – evening,
    Beautiful, beautiful Soup!

Beautiful Soup! Who cares for fish,
Game, or any other dish?
Who would not give all else for two
pennyworth only of Beautiful Soup?
Pennyworth only of beautiful Soup?
    Beau – ootiful Soo – oop!
    Beau – ootiful Soo – oop!
Soo – oop of the e – e – evening,
    Beautiful, beauti – FUL SOUP!

Lewis Carroll

THE WHITE KNIGHT'S SONG

I'll tell thee everything I can;
    There's little to relate.
I saw an aged aged man,
    A-sitting on a gate.
'Who are you, aged man?' I said,
    'And how is it you live?'
And his answer trickled through my head
    Like water through a sieve.

He said, 'I look for butterflies
    That sleep among the wheat:
I make them into mutton-pies,
    And sell them in the street.
I sell them unto men,' he said,
    'Who sail on stormy seas;
And that's the way I get my bread –
    A trifle; if you please.'

But I was thinking of a plan
    To dye one's whiskers green,
And always use so large a fan
    That they could not be seen.
So, having no reply to give
    To what the old man said,
I cried, 'Come, tell me how you live!'
    And thumped him on the head.

His accents mild took up the tale:
    He said, 'I go my ways,
And when I find a mountain-rill,
    I set it in a blaze;
And thence they make a stuff they call
    Rowlands' Macassar Oil –
Yet twopence-halfpenny is all
    They give me for my toil.'

But I was thinking of a way
    To feed oneself on batter,
And so go on from day to day
    Getting a little fatter.
I shook him well from side to side,
    Until his face was blue:
'Come, tell me how you live,' I cried,
    'And what it is you do!'

He said, 'I hunt for haddocks' eyes
    Among the heather bright,
And work them into waistcoat-buttons
    In the silent night.
And these I do not sell for gold
    Or coin of silvery shine,
But for a copper halfpenny,
    And that will purchase nine.

'I sometimes dig for buttered rolls,
    Or set limed twigs for crabs;
I sometimes search the grassy knolls
    For wheels of Hansom-cabs.
And that's the way' (he gave a wink)
    'By which I get my wealth –
And very gladly will I drink
    Your Honour's noble health.'

I heard him then, for I had just
    Completed my design
To keep the Menai bridge from rust
    By boiling it in wine.
I thanked him much for telling me
    The way he got his wealth,
But chiefly for his wish that he
    Might drink my noble health.

And now, if e'er by chance I put
    My fingers into glue,
Or madly squeeze a right-hand foot
    Into a left-hand shoe,
Or if I drop upon my toe
    A very heavy weight,
I weep, for it reminds me so
    Of that old man I used to know –

Whose look was mild, whose speech was slow,
Whose hair was whiter than the snow,
Whose face was very like a crow,
With eyes, like cinders, all aglow,
Who seemed distracted with his woe,
Who rocked his body to and fro,
And muttered mumblingly and low,
As if his mouth were full of dough,
Who snorted like a buffalo –
That summer evening long ago
    A-sitting on a gate.

Lewis Carroll

THE WALRUS AND THE CARPENTER

The sun was shining on the sea,
    Shining with all his might:
He did his very best to make
    The billows smooth and bright –
And this was odd, because it was
    The middle of the night.

The moon was shining sulkily,
    Because she thought the sun
Had got no business to be there
    After the day was done –
'It's very rude of him,' she said,
    'To come and spoil the fun!'

The sea was wet as wet could be,
　　The sands were dry as dry.
You could not see a cloud, because
　　No cloud was in the sky:
No birds were flying overhead –
　　There were no birds to fly.

The Walrus and the Carpenter
　　Were walking close at hand;
They wept like anything to see
　　Such quantities of sand:
'If this were only cleared away,'
　　They said, 'it *would* be grand!'

'If seven maids with seven mops
　　Swept it for half a year,
Do you suppose,' the Walrus said,
　　'That they could get it clear?'
'I doubt it,' said the Carpenter,
　　And shed a bitter tear.

'O Oysters, come and walk with us!'
　　The Walrus did beseech.
'A pleasant walk, a pleasant talk,
　　Along the briny beach:
We cannot do with more than four,
　　To give a hand to each.'

Lewis Carroll

The eldest Oyster looked at him,
    But never a word he said:
The eldest Oyster winked his eye,
    And shook his heavy head –
Meaning to say he did not choose
    To leave the oyster-bed.

But four young Oysters hurried up,
    All eager for the treat:
Their coats were brushed, their faces washed,
    Their shoes were clean and neat –
And this was odd, because, you know,
    They hadn't any feet.

Four other Oysters followed them,
    And yet another four;
And thick and fast they came at last,
    And more, and more, and more –
All hopping through the frothy waves,
    And scrambling to the shore.

The Walrus and the Carpenter
    Walked on a mile or so,
And then they rested on a rock
    Conveniently low:
And all the little Oysters stood
    And waited in a row.

The time has come,' the Walrus said,
    'To talk of many things:
Of shoes – and ships – and sealing-wax –
    Of cabbages – and kings –
And why the sea is boiling hot –
    And whether pigs have wings.'

'But wait a bit,' the Oysters cried,
    'Before we have our chat;
For some of us are out of breath,
    And all of us are fat!'
'No hurry!' said the Carpenter.
    They thanked him much for that.

'A loaf of bread,' the Walrus said,
    'Is what we chiefly need:
Pepper and vinegar besides
    Are very good indeed –
Now if you're ready, Oysters dear,
    We can begin to feed.'

'But not on us!' the Oysters cried,
    Turning a little blue.
'After such kindness, that would be
    A dismal thing to do!'
'The night is fine,' the Walrus said.
    'Do you admire the view?

'It was so kind of you to come!
    And you are very nice!'
The Carpenter said nothing but
    'Cut us another slice:
I wish you were not quite so deaf –
    I've had to ask you twice!'

'It seems a shame,' the Walrus said,
    'To play them such a trick,
After we've brought them out so far,
    And made them trot so quick!'
The Carpenter said nothing but
    'The butter's spread too thick!'

'I weep for you,' the Walrus said:
    'I deeply sympathize.'
With sobs and tears he sorted out
    Those of the largest size,
Holding his pocket-handkerchief
    Before his streaming eyes.

'O Oysters,' said the Carpenter,
    'You've had a pleasant run!
Shall we be trotting home again?'
    But answer came there none —
And this was scarcely odd, because
    They'd eaten every one.

FATHER WILLIAM

'You are old, Father William,' the young man said,
    'And your hair has become very white;
And yet you incessantly stand on your head –
    Do you think, at your age, it is right?'

'In my youth,' Father William replied to his son,
    'I feared it might injure the brain;
But, now that I'm perfectly sure I have none,
    Why, I do it again and again.'

'You are old,' said the youth, 'as I mentioned before,
    And have grown most uncommonly fat;
Yet you turned a back-somersault in at the door –
    Pray, what is the reason of that?'

'In my youth,' said the sage, as he shook his grey locks,
    'I kept all my limbs very supple
By the use of this ointment – one shilling the box –
    Allow me to sell you a couple?'

'You are old,' said the youth, 'and your jaws are too weak
    For anything tougher than suet;
Yet you finished the goose, with the bones and the beak –
    Pray, how did you manage to do it?'

'In my youth,' said his father, 'I took to the law,
    And argued each case with my wife;
And the muscular strength, which it gave to my jaw,
    Has lasted the rest of my life.'

'You are old,' said the youth, 'one would hardly suppose
    That your eye was as steady as ever;
Yet you balanced an eel on the end of your nose –
    What made you so awfully clever?'

'I have answered three questions, and that is enough,'
    Said his father, 'don't give yourself airs!
Do you think I can listen all day to such stuff?
    Be off, or I'll kick you down-stairs!'

Anonymous

OUR YAK

We are very depressed with our yak,
Which has now become terribly slak.
It cleaned kitchens and stairs
Better than many au pairs,
But now we're going to send our yak bak.

G.K. Chesterton

THE ONENESS
OF THE PHILOSOPHER
WITH NATURE

I love to see the little stars
    All dancing to one tune;
I think quite highly of the Sun,
    and kindly of the Moon.

G.K. Chesterton

The million forests of the Earth
Come trooping in to tea.
The great Niagara waterfall
Is never shy with me.

I am the tiger's confidant,
 And never mention names:
The lion drops the formal 'Sir',
 And lets me call him James.

Into my ear the blushing Whale
Stammers his love. I know
Why the Rhinoceros is sad,
  – Ah, child! 'twas long ago.

G.K. Chesterton

I am akin to all the Earth
   By many a tribal sign:
The aged Pig will often wear
   That sad, sweet smile of mine.

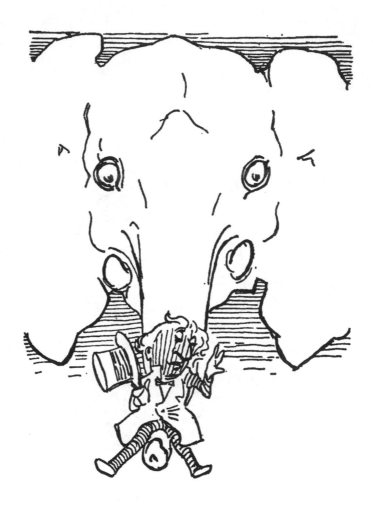

My niece, the Barnacle, has got
My piercing eyes of black;
The Elephant has got my nose,
I do not want it back.

G.K. Chesterton

I know the strange tale of the Slug;
    The Early Sin – the Fall –
The Sleep – the Vision – and the Vow –
    The Quest – the Crown – the Call.

G.K. *Chesterton*

And I have loved the Octopus,
　Since we were boys together.
I love the Vulture and the Shark:
　I even love the weather.

I love to bask in sunny fields,
    And when that hope is vain,
I go and bask in Baker Street,
    All in the pouring rain.

Come snow! where fly, by some strange law,
  Hard snowballs – without noise –
Through streets untenanted, except
  By good unconscious boys.

Come fog! Exultant mystery –
    Where, in strange darkness rolled,
The end of my own nose becomes
    A lovely legend old.

G.K. Chesterton

Come snow, and hail, and thunderbolts,
　Sleet, fire, and general fuss;
Come to my arms, come all at once –
　Oh photograph me thus!

KIPH

My Uncle Ben, who's been
To Bisk, Bhir, Biak –
Been, and come back:
To Tab, Tau, Tze, and Tomsk,
And home, by Teneriffe:
Who, brown as desert sand,
Gaunt, staring, slow and stiff,
Has chased the Unicorn
And Hippogriff,
Gave me a smooth, small, shining stone,
Called *Kiph*.

'Look'ee, now, Nevvy mine,'
He told me – '*If*
You'd wish a wish,
Just rub this smooth, small, shining stone,
Called *Kiph*.'

Hide it did I,
In a safe, secret spot;
Slept, and the place
In dreams forgot.

One wish *alone*
Now's mine: Oh, if
I could but find again
That stone called *Kiph*!

THE ELEPHANT IS A GRACEFUL BIRD

The elephant is a graceful bird;
  It flits from twig to twig.
It builds its nest in a rhubarb tree
  And whistles like a pig.

MOTHER, SAYING ANNE GOOD NIGHT

Mother, saying Anne good night,
Feared the dark would cause her fright.
'Four angels guard you,' low she said,
'One at the foot and one at the head –'

'Mother – quick – the pillow!! – There!!!
Missed that angel, skimmed his hair.
Never mind, we'll get the next.
Ooh! but angels make me vexed!!'

Mother, shocked, gasped feebly 'Anne!!!'
(A pillow disabled the water-can.)
Said Anne, 'I won't have things in white
Chant prayers about my bed all night.'

James Fenton

THIS OCTOPUS EXPLOITS WOMEN

Even the barnacle has certain rights
The grim anemones should not ignore,
And the gay bivalves in their fishnet tights
Are linking arms with fins to ask for maw.

The hectic round of rockpools is disrupted
By the addresses of the finny vicars,
With which the limpet choirboys were corrupted.
The knitting-fish produce their eight leg knickers

While somewhere in the depths a voice keeps shouting:
'By Jove! that was a narrow bathyscaphe.'
What made the Junior Sea-Slugs give up scouting?
The *Daily Seaweed* tells us nowhere's safe.

Beneath the shimmering surface of the ocean,
The thoroughfare of ketches, sloops and luggers,
With their thick boots and hair smothered in lotion,
Are gathering hordes of ruthless ichthic muggers.

The workers on the derricks live in terror.
You can't stroll out across the sea at night.
Professor Walrus writes (see *Drowned in Error*):
'The lemon sole are taught to shoot on sight.'

The lobsters at the water polo club
Sip their prawn cocktails, chatting over chukkas.
The octopus rests idly in its tub.
The Tunny Girls are lounging on its suckers.

123

A FARMER WENT TROTTING

A farmer went trotting upon his grey mare,
    Bumpety, bumpety bump!
With his daughter behind him so rosy and fair,
    Lumpety, lumpety, lump!

A raven cried, Croak! And they all tumbled down,
    Bumpety, bumpety, bump!
The mare broke her knees and the farmer his crown,
    Lumpety, lumpety, lump!

The mischievous raven flew laughing away,
    Bumpety, bumpety, bump!
And vowed he would serve them the same the next day,
    Lumpety, lumpety, lump!

Anonymous

THE KING SAID TO SALOME

The King said to Salome,
  'We'll have no dancing here!'
Salome said, 'The heck with you!'
  And kicked the chandelier.

126

Edward Gorey

THE UTTER ZOO ALPHABET

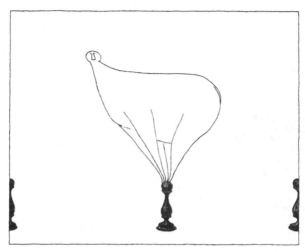

The Ampoo is intensely neat;
Its head is small, likewise its feet.

The Boggerslosh conceals itself
In back of bottles on a shelf.

128

Edward Gorey

The Crunk is not unseldom drastic
And must be hindered by elastic.

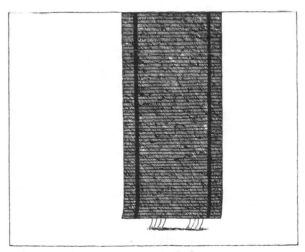

The Dawbis is remote and shy;
It shuns the gaze of passers-by.

The Epitwee's inclined to fits
Until at last it falls to bits.

The Fidknop is devoid of feeling;
It drifts about beneath the ceiling.

The Gawdge is understood to save
All sorts of objects in its cave.

The Humglum crawls along the ground,
And never makes the slightest sound.

Edward Gorey

The Ippagoggy has a taste
For every kind of glue and paste.

The Jelbislup cannot get far
Because it's kept inside a jar.

132

The Kwongdzu has enormous claws;
Its character is full of flaws.

The Limpflig finds it hard to keep
From spending all its life asleep.

The Mork proceeds with pensive grace
And no expression on its face.

The Neapse's sufferings are chronic;
It lives exclusively on tonic.

The Ombledroom is vast and white,
And therefore visible by night.

The Posby goes into a trance
In which it does a little dance.

The Quingawaga squeaks and moans
While dining off of ankle bones.

The Raitch hangs downward from its tail
By knotting it around a nail.

The Scrug's extremely nasty-looking,
And is unusable for cooking.

The Twibbit on occasion knows
A difficulty with its toes.

The Ulp is very, very small;
It hardly can be seen at all.

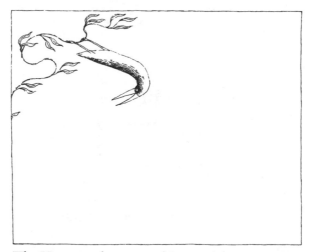

The Veazy makes a creaking noise;
It has no dignity or poise.

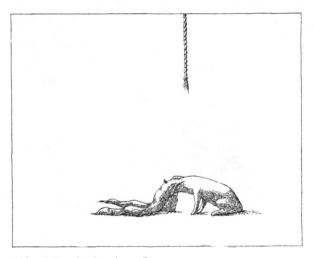

The Wambulus has floppy ears
With which to wipe away its tears.

The Xyke stands up at close of day,
And then it slowly walks away.

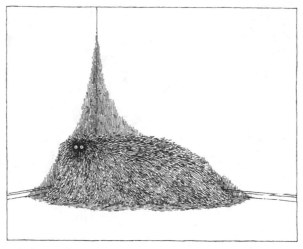

The Yawfle stares, and stares, and stares,
And stares, and stares, and stares, and stares.

About the Zote what can be said?
There was just one, and now it's dead.

Edward Gorey

THE OSBICK BIRD

Edward Gorey

An osbick bird flew down and sat
On Emblus Fingby's bowler hat.

It had not done so for a whim,
But meant to come and live with him.

142

On Fridays Emblus played the flute;
The bird now joined him on a lute.

The top of the zagava tree
Was frequently where they had tea.

Edward Gorey

They sometimes strolled beyond the town
In time to watch the sun go down.

The cards got battered past repair
As they played double solitaire.

And after that they would not speak
To one another for a week.

They went to Periboo by car
And places twice again as far.

In winter they were both discreet
And wore galoshes on their feet.

Upon the river Oad the two
Were often seen in their canoe.

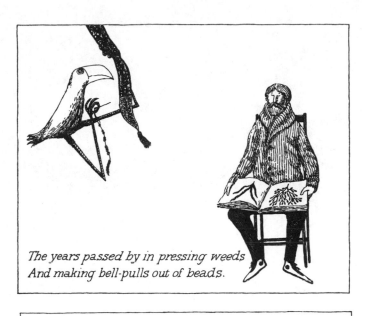

*The years passed by in pressing weeds
And making bell-pulls out of beads.*

*And when at last poor Emblus died
The osbick bird was by his side.*

He was interred; the bird alone
Was left to sit upon his stone.

But after several months, one day
It changed its mind and flew away.

Edward Gorey

THE UNTITLED BOOK

[The Untitled Book]

Hippity wippity,

Oxiborick;

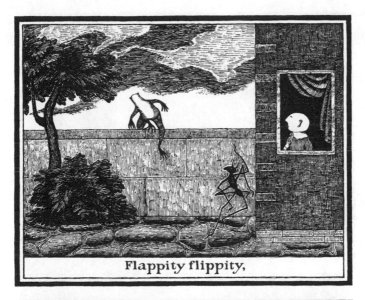

Flappity flippity,

Saragashum;

Edward Gorey

Thip,

thap,

152

thoo.

Thumbleby stumbleby,

Ipsifendus;

Rambleby rumbleby,

Quoggenzocker;

Hip,

Edward Gorey

hop,

hoo.

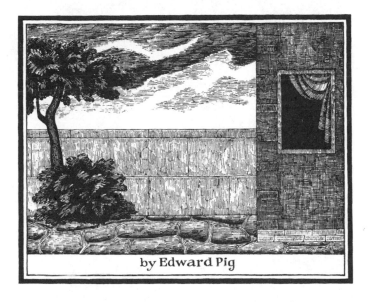

by Edward Pig

PATIENCE

When skiing in the Engadine
My hat blew off down a ravine.
My son, who went to fetch it back,
Slipped through an icy glacier's crack
And then got permanently stuck.

It really was infernal luck:
My hat was practically new –
I loved my little Henry too –
And I may have to wait for years
Till either of them reappears.

Harry Graham

THE FOND FATHER

Of Baby I was very fond,
She'd won her father's heart;
So, when she fell into the pond,
It gave me quite a start.

Harry Graham

THE PERILS OF OBESITY

Yesterday my gun exploded
When I thought it wasn't loaded;
Near my wife I pressed the trigger,
Chipped a fragment off her figure.
'Course I'm sorry, and all that,
But she shouldn't be so fat.

GRANDPAPA

Grandpapa fell down a drain;
Couldn't scramble out again.
Now he's floating down the sewer
There's one grandpapa the fewer.

HIGH DIDDLE DIDDLE

High diddle diddle,
The cat and the fiddle,
 The cow jump'd over the moon;
The little dog laugh'd
To see such craft,
 And the dish ran away with the spoon.

Ted Hughes

WODWO

What am I? Nosing here, turning leaves over
Following a faint stain on the air to the river's edge
I enter water. What am I to split
The glassy grain of water looking upward I see the bed
Of the river above me upside down very clear
What am I doing here in mid-air? Why do I find
this frog so interesting as I inspect its most secret
interior and make it my own? Do these weeds
know me and name me to each other have they
seen me before, do I fit in their world? I seem
separate from the ground and not rooted but dropped
out of nothing casually I've no threads
fastening me to anything I can go anywhere
I seem to have been given the freedom
of this place what am I then? And picking
bits of bark off this rotten stump gives me
no pleasure and it's no use so why do I do it
me and doing that have coincided very queerly
But what shall I be called am I the first
have I an owner what shape am I what
shape am I am I huge if I go
to the end on this way past these trees and past these trees
till I get tired that's touching one wall of me
for the moment if I sit still how everything
stops to watch me I suppose I am the exact centre
but there's all this what is it roots
roots roots roots and here's the water
again very queer but I'll go on looking

Anonymous

I HAD A LITTLE HUSBAND

I had a little husband
    No bigger than my thumb;
I put him in a pint pot
    And there I bid him drum.
I gave him some garters
    To garter up his hose,
And a little silk handkerchief
    To wipe his pretty nose.

I PUT MY HAT UPON MY HEAD

I put my hat upon my head
 And walk'd into the Strand,
And there I met another man
 Whose hat was in his hand.

IF THE MAN WHO TURNEPS CRIES

If the man who Turneps cries
Cry not when his Father dies;
'Tis a sign that he had rather
Have a Turnep than a Father.

THE OWL AND THE PUSSY-CAT

The Owl and the Pussy-cat went to sea
    In a beautiful pea-green boat,
They took some honey, and plenty of money,
    Wrapped up in a five-pound note.
The Owl looked up to the stars above,
    And sang to a small guitar,
'O lovely Pussy! O Pussy, my love,
    What a beautiful Pussy you are,
        You are,
        You are!
What a beautiful Pussy you are!'

Pussy said to the Owl, 'You elegant fowl!
  How charmingly sweet you sing!
O let us be married! too long we have tarried:
  But what shall we do for a ring?'
They sailed away, for a year and a day,
  To the land where the Bong-tree grows,
And there in a wood a Piggy-wig stood
  With a ring at the end of his nose,
    His nose,
    His nose,
With a ring at the end of his nose.

'Dear Pig, are you willing to sell for one shilling
  Your ring?' Said the Piggy, 'I will.'
So they took it away, and were married next day
  By the Turkey who lives on the hill.
They dined on mince, and slices of quince,
  Which they ate with a runcible spoon;
And hand in hand, on the edge of the sand,
  They danced by the light of the moon,
    The moon,
    The moon,
They danced by the light of the moon.

Edward Lear

THE POBBLE WHO HAS NO TOES

The Pobble who has no toes
    Had once as many as we;
When they said 'Some day you may lose them all;'–
    He replied, – 'Fish fiddle-de-dee!'
And his Aunt Jobiska made him drink,
Lavender water tinged with pink,
For she said, 'The World in general knows
    There's nothing so good for a Pobble's toes!'

The Pobble who has no toes,
    Swam across the Bristol Channel;
But before he set out he wrapped his nose,
    In a piece of scarlet flannel.
For his Aunt Jobiska said, 'No harm
Can come to his toes if his nose is warm;
And it's perfectly known that a Pobble's toes
Are safe, – provided he minds his nose!'

The Pobble swam fast and well
    And when boats or ships came near him
He tinkledy-binkledy-winkled a bell
    So that all the world could hear him.
And all the Sailors and Admirals cried,
When they saw him nearing the further side, –
'He has gone to fish for his Aunt Jobiska's
Runcible Cat with crimson whiskers!'

But before he touched the shore,
    The shore of the Bristol Channel,
A sea-green Porpoise carried away
    His wrapper of scarlet flannel.
And when he came to observe his feet
Formerly garnished with toes so neat
His face at once became forlorn
On perceiving that all his toes were gone!

And nobody ever knew
    From that dark day to the present,
Whoso had taken the Pobble's toes,
    In a manner so far from pleasant.
Whether the shrimps or crawfish grey,
Or crafty Mermaids stole them away –
Nobody knew; and nobody knows
How the Pobble was robbed of his twice five toes!

The Pobble who has no toes
    Was placed in a friendly Bark,
And they rowed him back, and carried him up,
    To his Aunt Jobiska's Park.
And she made him a feast at his earnest wish
Of eggs and buttercups fried with fish; –
And she said,- 'It's a fact the whole world knows,
That Pobbles are happier without their toes!'

THE JUMBLIES

They went to sea in a Sieve, they did,
    In a Sieve they went to sea:
In spite of all their friends could say,
On a winter's morn, on a stormy day,
    In a Sieve they went to sea!
And when the Sieve turned round and round,
And every one cried, 'You'll all be drowned!'
They called aloud, 'Our Sieve ain't big,
But we don't care a button! we don't care a fig!
    In a Sieve we'll go to sea!'
      Far and few, far and few,
        Are the lands where the Jumblies live;
      Their heads are green, and their hands are blue,
        And they went to sea in a Sieve.

They sailed away in a Sieve, they did,
    In a Sieve they sailed so fast,
With only a beautiful pea-green veil
Tied with a ribbon by way of a sail,
    To a small tobacco-pipe mast;
And every one said, who saw them go,
'O won't they be soon upset, you know!
For the sky is dark, and the voyage is long,
And happen what may, it's extremely wrong
    In a Sieve to sail so fast!'
      Far and few, far and few,
        Are the lands where the Jumblies live;
      Their heads are green, and their hands are blue,
        And they went to sea in a Sieve.

171

Edward Lear

The water it soon came in, it did,
    The water it soon came in;
So to keep them dry, they wrapped their feet
In a pinky paper all folded neat,
    And they fastened it down with a pin.
And they passed the night in a crockery-jar,
And each of them said, 'How wise we are!
Though the sky be dark, and the voyage be long,
Yet we never can think we were rash or wrong,
    While round in our Sieve we spin!'
        Far and few, far and few,
            Are the lands where the Jumblies live;
            Their heads are green, and their hands are blue,
            And they went to sea in a Sieve.

And all night long they sailed away;
    And when the sun went down,
They whistled and warbled a moony song
To the echoing sound of a coppery gong,
    In the shade of the mountains brown.
'O Timballoo! How happy we are,
    When we live in a Sieve and a crockery-jar,
And all night long in the moonlight pale,
We sail away with a pea-green sail,
    In the shade of the mountains brown!'
        Far and few, far and few,
            Are the lands where the Jumblies live;
            Their heads are green, and their hands are blue,
            And they went to sea in a Sieve.

172

They sailed to the Western Sea, they did,
    To a land all covered with trees,
And they bought an Owl, and a useful Cart,
And a pound of Rice, and a Cranberry Tart,
    And a hive of silvery Bees.
And they bought a Pig, and some green Jack-daws,
And a lovely Monkey with lollipop paws,
And forty bottles of Ring-Bo-Ree,
    And no end of Stilton Cheese.
        Far and few, far and few,
            Are the lands where the Jumblies live;
        Their heads are green, and their hands are blue,
            And they went to sea in a Sieve.

And in twenty years they all came back,
    In twenty years or more,
And every one said, 'How tall they've grown!
For they've been to the Lakes, and the Torrible Zone,
    And the hills of the Chankly Bore!'
And they drank their health, and gave them a feast
Of dumplings made of beautiful yeast;
And every one said, 'If we only live,
We too will go to sea in a Sieve,–
    To the hills of the Chankly Bore!'
        Far and few, far and few,
            Are the lands where the Jumblies live;
        Their heads are green, and their hands are blue,
            And they went to sea in a Sieve.

Edward Lear

THE AKOND OF SWAT

Who, or why, or which, or what, Is the Akond of SWAT?
Is he tall or short, or dark or fair?
Does he sit on a stool or a sofa or a chair,   or SQUAT,
                     The Akond of Swat?

Is he wise or foolish, young or old?
Does he drink his soup and his coffee cold,   or HOT,
                     The Akond of Swat?

Does he sing or whistle, jabber or talk,
And when riding abroad does he gallop or walk,   or TROT
                     The Akond of Swat?

Does he wear a turban, a fez, or a hat?
Does he sleep on a mattress, a bed, or a mat,   or a COT,
                     The Akond of Swat?

When he writes a copy in round-hand size,
Does he cross his T's and finish his I's   with a DOT,
                     The Akond of Swat?

Can he write a letter concisely clear
Without a speck or a smudge or smear   or BLOT,
                     The Akond of Swat?

Do his people like him extremely well?
Or do they, whenever they can, rebel,   or PLOT
                     The Akond of Swat?

If he catches them then, either old or young,
Does he have them chopped in pieces or hung,   or SHOT
                                    The Akond of Swat?

Do his people prig in the lanes or park?
Or even at times, when days are dark,   GAROTTE?
                                    O the Akond of Swat!

Does he study the wants of his own dominion?
Or doesn't he care for public opinion   a JOT,
                                    The Akond of Swat?

To amuse his mind do his people show him
Pictures, or any one's last new poem,   or WHAT,
                                    For the Akond of Swat?

At night if he suddenly screams and wakes,
Do they bring him only a few small cakes,   or a LOT,
                                    For the Akond of Swat?

Does he live on turnips, tea, or tripe?
Does he like his shawl to be marked with a stripe,   or a DOT,
                                    The Akond of Swat?

Does he like to lie on his back in a boat
Like the lady who lived in that isle remote,   SHALLOTT,
                                    The Akond of Swat?

Edward Lear

Is he quiet, or always making a fuss?
Is his steward a Swiss or a Swede or a Russ,   or a SCOT,
              The Akond of Swat?

Does he like to sit by the calm blue wave?
Or to sleep and snore in a dark green cave,   or a GROTT,
              The Akond of Swat?

Does he drink small beer from a silver jug?
Or a bowl? or a glass? or a cup? or a mug?   or a POT,
              The Akond of Swat?

Does he beat his wife with a gold-topped pipe,
When she lets the gooseberries grow too ripe,   or ROT,
              The Akond of Swat?

Does he wear a white tie when he dines with friends,
And tie it neat in a bow with ends,   or a KNOT,
              The Akond of Swat?

Does he like new cream, and hate mince-pies?
When he looks at the sun does he wink his eyes,   or NOT,
              The Akond of Swat?

Does he teach his subjects to roast and bake?
Does he sail about on an inland lake,   in a YACHT,
              The Akond of Swat?

Some one, or nobody, knows I wot
Who or which or why or what   Is the Akond of Swat!

INCIDENTS IN THE LIFE OF MY UNCLE ARLY

O! My agèd Uncle Arly!
Sitting on a heap of Barley
    Thro' the silent hours of night, –
Close beside a leafy thicket: –
On his nose there was a Cricket, –
In his hat a Railway-Ticket; –
    (But his shoes were far too tight.)

Long ago, in youth, he squander'd
All his goods away, and wander'd
    To the Tiniskoop-hills afar.
There on golden sunsets blazing,
Every morning found him gazing, –
Singing – 'Orb! you're quite amazing!
    How I wonder what you are!'

Like the ancient Medes and Persians,
Always by his own exertions
    He subsisted on those hills; –
Whiles, – by teaching children spelling, –
Or at times by merely yelling, –
Or at intervals by selling
    'Propter's Nicodemus Pills.'

Later, in his morning rambles
He perceived the moving brambles –
    Something square and white disclose; –
'Twas a First-class Railway-Ticket;
But, on stooping down to pick it
Off the ground, – a pea-green Cricket
    Settled on my uncle's Nose.

Never – never more, – oh! never,
Did that Cricket leave him ever, –
    Dawn or evening, day or night; –
Clinging as a constant treasure, –
Chirping with a cheerious measure, –
Wholly to my uncle's pleasure
    (Though his shoes were far too tight.)

So for three-and-forty winters,
Till his shoes were worn to splinters,
    Those hills he wander'd o'er, –
Sometimes silent; – sometimes yelling; –
Till he came to Borley-Melling,
Near his old ancestral dwelling; –
    (But his shoes were far too tight.)

On a little heap of Barley
Died my agèd uncle Arly,
    And they buried him one night; –
Close beside the leafy thicket; –
There, – his hat and Railway-Ticket; –
There, – his ever-faithful Cricket; –
    (But his shoes were far too tight.)

Edward Lear

CALICO PIE

Calico Pie,
  The little Birds fly
Down to the calico tree,
    Their wings were blue,
    And they sang 'Tilly-loo!'
    Till away they flew, –
And they never came back to me!
    They never came back!
    They never came back!
They never came back to me!

Calico Jam,
The little Fish swam,
Over the syllabub sea,
He took off his hat,
To the Sole and the Sprat,
And the Willeby-wat, –
But he never came back to me!
He never came back!
He never came back!
He never came back to me!

Calico Ban,
The little Mice ran,
To be ready in time for tea,
Flippity flup,
They drank it all up,
And danced in the cup, –
But they never came back to me!
They never came back!
They never came back!
They never came back to me!

Calico Drum,
The Grasshoppers come,
The Butterfly, Beetle, and Bee,
Over the ground,
Around and round,
With a hop and a bound, –
But they never came back!
They never came back!
They never came back!
They never came back to me!

THE QUANGLE WANGLE'S HAT

On the top of the Crumpetty Tree
    The Quangle Wangle sat,
But his face you could not see,
    On account of his Beaver Hat.
For his Hat was a hundred and two feet wide,
    With ribbons and bibbons on every side
And bells, and buttons, and loops, and lace,
    So that nobody ever could see the face
    Of the Quangle Wangle Quee.

The Quangle Wangle said
　　To himself on the Crumpetty Tree, –
'Jam; and jelly; and bread;
　　'Are the best food for me!
'But the longer I live on this Crumpetty Tree
'The plainer that ever it seems to me
'That very few people come this way
'And that life on the whole is far from gay!'
　　Said the Quangle Wangle Quee.

But there came to the Crumpetty Tree,
    Mr and Mrs Canary;
And they said, – 'Did you ever see
    'Any spot so charmingly airy?
'May we build a nest on your lovely Hat?
'Mr Quangle Wangle, grant us that!
'O please let us come and build a nest
'Of whatever material suits you best,
    'Mr Quangle Wangle Quee!'

And besides, to the Crumpetty Tree
    Came the Stork, the Duck, and the Owl;
The Snail, and the Bumble-Bee,
    The Frog, and the Fimble Fowl;
    (The Fimble Fowl, with a Corkscrew leg);
And all of them said, – 'We humbly beg,
    'We may build our homes on your lovely Hat, –
    'Mr Quangle Wangle, grant us that!
    'Mr Quangle Wangle Quee!'

And the Golden Grouse came there,
    And the Pobble who has no toes, –
And the small Olympian bear, –
    And the Dong with a luminous nose.
And the Blue Baboon, who played the flute, –
And the Orient Calf from the Land of Tute, –
And the Attery Squash, and the Bisky Bat, –
All came and built on the lovely Hat
    Of the Quangle Wangle Quee.

And the Quangle Wangle said
    To himself on the Crumpetty Tree, –
'When all these creatures move
    'What a wonderful noise there'll be!'
And at night by the light of the Mulberry moon
They danced to the flute of the Blue Baboon,
On the broad green leaves of the Crumpetty Tree,
And all were as happy as happy could be,
    With the Quangle Wangle Quee.

Edward Lear

THERE WAS AN OLD MAN WITH A BEARD

There was an Old Man with a beard,
Who said, 'It is just as I feared! –
Two Owls and a Hen, four Larks and a Wren,
Have all built their nests in my beard!'

Edward Lear

THE DONG WITH A LUMINOUS NOSE

When awful darkness and silence reign
Over the great Gromboolian plain,
   Through the long, long wintry nights; –
When the angry breakers roar
As they beat on the rocky shore; –
   When Storm-clouds brood on the towering heights
Of the Hills of the Chankly Bore: –

Then, through the vast and gloomy dark,
There moves what seems a fiery spark,
   A lonely spark with silvery rays
   Piercing the coal-black night, –
   A Meteor strange and bright: –
Hither and thither the vision strays,
   A single lurid light.

Slowly it wanders, – pauses, – creeps, –
Anon it sparkles, – flashes and leaps;
And ever as onward it gleaming goes
A light on the Bong-tree stem it throws.
And those who watch at that midnight hour
From Hall or Terrace, or lofty Tower,
Cry, as the wild light passes along, –
     'The Dong! – the Dong!
  'The wandering Dong through the forest goes!
     'The Dong! – the Dong!
  'The Dong with a luminous Nose!'

Long years ago
The Dong was happy and gay,
Till he fell in love with a Jumbly Girl
Who came to those shores one day,
For the Jumblies came in a sieve, they did, –
Landing at eve near the Zemmery Fidd
Where the Oblong Oysters grow,
And the rocks are smooth and grey.
And all the woods and the valleys rang
With the Chorus they daily and nightly sang, –
'Far and few, far and few,
Are the lands where the Jumblies live;
Their heads are green, and their hands are blue
And they went to sea in a sieve.'

Happily, happily passed those days!
While the cheerful Jumblies staid;
They danced in circlets all night long,
To the plaintive pipe of the lively Dong,
In moonlight, shine, or shade.
For day and night he was always there
By the side of the Jumbly Girl so fair,
With her sky-blue hands, and her sea-green hair.
Till the morning came of that hateful day
When the Jumblies sailed in their sieve away,
And the Dong was left on the cruel shore

Gazing – gazing for evermore, –
Ever keeping his weary eyes on
That pea-green sail on the far horizon, –
Singing the Jumbly Chorus still
As he sate all day on the grassy hill, –
  'Far and few, far and few,
  Are the lands where the Jumblies live;
  Their heads are green, and their hands are blue
  And they went to sea in a sieve.'

But when the sun was low in the West,
  The Dong arose and said; –
– 'What little sense I once possessed
  Has quite gone out of my head!' –
And since that day he wanders still
By lake and forest, marsh and hill,
Singing – 'O somewhere, in valley or plain
'Might I find my Jumbly Girl again!
For ever I'll seek by lake and shore
'Till I find my Jumbly Girl once more!'

Playing a pipe with silvery squeaks,
  Since then his Jumbly Girl he seeks,
  And because by night he could not see,
  He gathered the bark of the Twangum Tree
    On the flowery plain that grows.
    And he wove him a wondrous Nose, –
A Nose as strange as a Nose could be!

Of vast proportions and painted red,
And tied with cords to the back of his head.
  – In a hollow rounded space it ended
  With a luminous Lamp within suspended,
    All fenced about
    With a bandage stout
    To prevent the wind from blowing it out; –
  And with holes all round to send the light,
  In gleaming rays on the dismal night.

And now each night, and all night long,
Over those plains still roams the Dong;
And above the wail of the Chimp and Snipe
You may hear the squeak of his plaintive pipe
While ever he seeks, but seeks in vain
To meet with his Jumbly Girl again;
Lonely and wild – all night he goes, –
The Dong with a luminous Nose!
And all who watch at the midnight hour,
From Hall or Terrace, or lofty Tower,
Cry, as they trace the Meteor bright,
Moving along through the dreary night, –
    'This is the hour when forth he goes,
    'The Dong with a luminous Nose!
    'Yonder – over the plain he goes;
      'He goes!
      'He goes;
    'The Dong with a luminous Nose!'

UNCLE BRAM

Uncle Bram
a batcatcher of distinction
scorned the use of
battraps, batnets and batpoison.
'Newfangled nonsense,'
he would scoff, and off
he would go
to hang upside down

in the hope of snatching
one of the little bastards.

KUNG FU LEE

Kung Fu Lee
a greenbelt
with a reputation second to none
was more than vexed
when annexed
and one morning built upon.

Roger McGough

COUSIN FOSBURY

Cousin Fosbury
took his highjumping seriously.
To ensure a floppier flop
he consulted a contortionist
and had his vertebrae removed
by a backstreet vertebraeortionist.

Now he clears 8 foot with ease
and sleeps with his head
tucked under his knees.

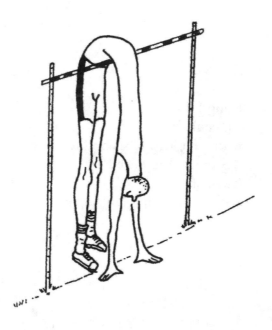

Roger McGough

ELMER HOOVER

Elmer Hoover
on vac from Vancouver
went fishing
off the Pier Head.

He caught 2 dead rats
dysentery
and a shoal of slimywhite balloonthings
which he brought home in a jamjar.
'Mersey cod,' we told him.

So he took the biggest
back to Canada.
Had it stuffed, mounted,
and displayed over the fireplace
in his trophy room.

'But you shudda seen
the one that got away,'
he would say.
Nonplussing his buddies.

Roger McGough

ENO

To be a sumo wrestler
    It pays to be fat.
'Nonsense,' said Eno,
    'I don't believe that.'

So he took his skinny
    little frame
to Tokyo
    in search of fame.

But even with God on
    his side
Eno got trod on
    and died.

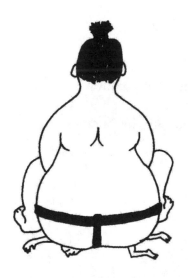

196

WILD BILL SITTING BULL

Wild Bill Sitting Bull
(half cowboy, half Sioux)
confused by watching Westerns
went in search of caribou.

In the Badlands
he was strangled
by his spangled lasso

Did a wardance
then scalped himself
like a man's gotta do.

Anonymous

LITTLE BLUE BEN

Little Blue Ben,
    who lives in the glen,
Keeps a blue cat
    and one blue hen.

Anonymous

Which lays of blue eggs
    a score and ten;
Where shall I find
    the little Blue Ben?

Spike Milligan

A THOUSAND HAIRY SAVAGES

A thousand hairy savages
Sitting down to lunch
Gobble gobble glup glup
Munch munch munch.

Spike Milligan

HIPPORHINOSTRICOW

Such a beast is the Hipporhinostricow
How it got so mixed up we'll never know how;
It sleeps all day, and whistles all night,
And it wears yellow socks which are far too tight.

If you laugh at the Hipporhinostricow,
You're bound to get into an awful row;
The creature is protected you see
From silly people like you and me.

Spike Milligan

CAN A PARROT

Can a parrot
Eat a carrot
Standing on his head?
If I did that my mum would send me
Straight upstairs to bed.

ON THE NING NANG NONG

On the Ning Nang Nong
Where the Cows go Bong!
and the Monkeys all say Boo!
There's a Nong Nang Ning
Where the trees go Ping!
And the tea pots Jibber Jabber Joo.
On the Nong Ning Nang
All the mice go Clang!
And you just can't catch 'em when they do!
So it's Ning Nang Nong!
Cows go Bong!
Nong Nang Ning!
Trees go Ping !
Nong Ning Nang!
The mice go Clang!
What a noisy place to belong,
is the Ning Nang Ning Nang Nong!!

Spike Milligan

THE LAND OF THE BUMBLEY BOO

In the Land of the Bumbley Boo
The people are red white and blue,
They never blow noses,
Or ever wear closes,
What a sensible thing to do!

In the Land of the Bumbley Boo
You can buy Lemon pie at the Zoo;
They give away Foxes
In little Pink Boxes
And Bottles of Dandylion Stew.

In the Land of the Bumbley Boo
You never see a Gnu,
But thousands of cats
Wearing trousers and hats
Made of Pumpkins and Pelican Glue!

Chorus
Oh, the Bumbley Boo! the Bumbley Boo!
That's the place for me and you!
So hurry! Let's run!
The train leaves at one!
For the Land of the Bumbley Boo!
The wonderful Bumbley Boo-Boo-Boo!
The wonderful Bumbley BOO!!!

MAVERIC

Maveric Prowles
Had Rumbling Bowles
That thundered in the night.
It shook the bedrooms all around
And gave the folks a fright.

The doctor called;
He was appalled
When through his stethoscope
He heard the sound of a baying hound,
And the acrid smell of smoke.

Was there a cure?
'The higher the fewer,'
The learned doctor said,
Then turned poor Maveric inside out
And stood him on his head.

'Just as I thought
You've been and caught
An Asiatic flu –
You musn't go near dogs I fear
Unless they come near you.'

Poor Maveric cried.
He went cross-eyed,
His legs went green and blue.
The doctor hit him with a club
And charged him one and two.

And so my friend
This is the end,
A warning to the few:
Stay clear of doctors to the end
Or they'll get rid of you.

Spike Milligan

THE TWIT

Although the street
Was badly lit,
I distinctly
Saw a twit.
Though the light
Was very dim,
I think I saw
The whole of him.
The whole of him
Was shamrock-green:
He was the first twit
I had seen.
I said, I said:
'Are you a twit?'
And he said 'Yes –
So what of it?'

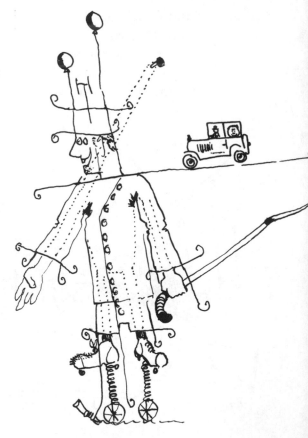

Spike Milligan

THE BONGALOO

'What is a Bongaloo, Daddy?'
'A Bongaloo, Son,' said I,
'Is a tall bag of cheese
Plus a Chinaman's knees
And the leg of a nanny goat's eye.'

'How strange is a Bongaloo, Daddy?'
'As strange as strange,' I replied.
'When the sun's in the West
It appears in a vest
Sailing out with the noonday tide.'

'What shape is a Bongaloo, Daddy?'
'The shape, my Son, I'll explain:
It's tall round the nose
Which continually grows
In the general direction of Spain.'

'Are you *sure* there's a Bongaloo, Daddy?'
'Am I sure, my Son?' said I.
'Why, I've seen it, not quite
On a dark sunny night
Do you think that I'd tell you a lie?'

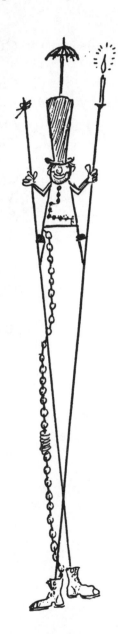

COTTLESTON PIE

Cottleston, Cottleston, Cottleston Pie,
A fly can't bird, but a bird can fly.
Ask me a riddle and I reply:
'*Cottleston, Cottleston, Cottleston Pie.*'

Cottleston, Cottleston, Cottleston Pie,
A fish can't whistle and neither can I.
Ask me a riddle and I reply:
'*Cottleston, Cottleston, Cottleston Pie.*'

Cottleston, Cottleston, Cottleston Pie,
Why does a chicken, I don't know why.
Ask me a riddle and I reply:
'*Cottleston, Cottleston, Cottleston Pie.*'

Anonymous

THE BOY STOOD ON THE BURNING DECK

The boy stood on the burning deck
Eating peanuts by the peck;
His father called him, he wouldn't go,
Because he loved the peanuts so.

AND ...

The boy stood on the burning deck,
His feet were full of blisters;
The flames came up and burned his pants,
And now he wears his sister's.

Ogden Nash

THE WOMBAT

The wombat lives across the seas,
Among the far Antipodes.
He may exist on nuts and berries,
Or then again, on missionaries;
His distant habitat precludes
Conclusive knowledge of his moods.
But I would not engage the wombat
In any form of mortal combat.

Ogden Nash

MUSTARD

I'm mad about mustard –
Even on custard.

Odgen Nash

THE PANDA

I love the Baby Giant Panda;
I'd welcome one to my veranda.
I never worry, wondering maybe
Whether it isn't Giant Baby;
I leave such matters to the scientists:
The Giant Baby – and Baby Giantists.
I simply wish a julep and a
Giant Baby Giant Panda.

Ogden Nash

THE OSTRICH

The ostrich roams the great Sahara.
Its mouth is wide, its neck is narra.
It has such long and lofty legs,
I'm glad it sits to lay its eggs.

Ogden Nash

THE HIPPOPOTAMUS

Behold the hippopotamus!
We laugh at how he looks to us,
And yet in moments dank and grim
I wonder how we look to him.
Peace, peace, thou hippopotamus!
We really look all right to us,
As you no doubt delight the eye
Of other hippotami.

THE GRACKLE

The grackle's voice is less than mellow,
His heart is black, his eye is yellow,
He bullies more attractive birds
With hoodlum deeds and vulgar words,
And should a human interfere,
Attacks that human in the rear.
I cannot help but deem the grackle
An ornithological debacle.

Mervyn Peake

O'ER SEAS THAT HAVE NO BEACHES

O'er seas that have no beaches
To end their waves upon,
I floated with twelve peaches,
A sofa and a swan.

The blunt waves crashed above us
The sharp waves burst around,
There was no one to love us,
No hope of being found –

Where, on the notched horizon
So endlessly a-drip,
I saw all of a sudden
No sign of any ship.

CROWN ME WITH HAIRPINS

Crown me with hairpins intertwined
Into a wreath each hairpin lined
With plush that only spinsters find
At night beneath huge sofas where
The feathers, wool and straw and hair
Bulge through a lining old as time
And secret as a beldam's lair
Of ghostly grime.

Tired aunts who live on sphagnum moss
Are quite the best to ask, because
They are less likely to get cross
Than those less ancient ones who still
Peer coyly from the window-sill,
Until their seventieth year.
Go find an old and *tired* one,
Secure the hairpin; then have done
With your relations, dear.

Mervyn Peake

OF PYGMIES, PALMS AND PIRATES

Of pygmies, palms and pirates,
Of islands and lagoons,
Of blood-bespotted frigates,
Of crags and octoroons,
Of whales and broken bottles,
Of quicksands cold and grey,
Of ullages and dottles,
I have no more to say.

Of barley, corn and furrows,
Of farms and turf that heaves
Above such ghostly burrows
As twitch on summer eves
Of fallow-land and pasture,
Of skies both pink and grey,
I made my statement last year
And have no more to say.

Mervyn Peake

I CANNOT GIVE THE REASONS

I cannot give the reasons,
I only sing the tunes:
the sadness of the seasons
the madness of the moons.

I cannot be didactic
or lucid, but I can
be quite obscure and practic-
ally marzipan.

In gorgery and gushness
and all that's squishified.
My voice has all the lushness
of what I can't abide.

And yet it has a beauty
most proud and terrible
denied to those whose duty
is to be cerebral.

Among the antlered mountains
I make my viscous way
and watch the sepia fountains
throw up their lime-green spray.

COME, BREAK THE NEWS TO ME, SWEET HORSE

'Come, break the news to me, Sweet Horse,
Do you not think it best?
Or if you'd rather not – of course
We'll let the matter rest.'

The biggest horse that ever wore
His waistcoat inside-out,
Replied: 'As I have sneezed before,
There's not a shade of doubt.'

'I find your answer rare, Sweet Horse,
Though hardly crystal-clear,
But tell me true, what kind of course
Do you propose to steer?'

The biggest horse that ever wore
His waistcoat outside-in,
Rolled over on the parquet floor
And kicked me on the chin

'O this is lovable,' I cried,
'And rather touching too,
Although I generally prefer
A lick of fish-bone glue.'

The only horse who ever kissed
Me smack athwart the chin
Curled up and died. He will be missed
By all who cherished him.

MIPS AND MA

Mips and ma the mooly moo,
The likes of him is biting who,
A cow's a care and who's a coo? –
What footie does is final.

My dearest dear my fairest fair,
Your father tossed a cat in air,
Though neither you nor I was there, –
What footie does is final.

Be large as an owl, be slick as a frog,
Be good as a goose, be big as a dog,
Be sleek as a heifer, be long as a hog, –
What footie will do will be final.

FESTE'S SONG

When that I was and a little tiny boy,
    With hey, ho, the wind and the rain,
A foolish thing was but a toy,
    For the rain it raineth every day.

But when I came to man's estate,
    With hey, ho, the wind and the rain,
'Gainst knaves and thieves men shut their gate,
    For the rain it raineth every day.

But when I came alas to wive,
    With hey, ho, the wind and the rain,
By swaggering could I never thrive,
    For the rain it raineth every day.

But when I came unto my beds,
    With hey, ho, the wind and the rain,
With toss-pots still had drunken heads,
    For the rain it raineth every day.

A great while ago the world begun,
    With hey, ho, the wind and the rain,
But that's all one, our play is done,
    And we'll strive to please you every day.

OH, MOTHER, I SHALL BE MARRIED

Oh, Mother,
 I shall be married
  To Mr Punchinello,
  To Mr Punch,
   To Mr Joe,

To Mr Nell,
To Mr Lo,
Mr Punch, Mr Joe,
Mr Nell, Mr Lo,
To Mr Punchinello!

MY HAT

Mother said if I wore this hat
I should be certain to get off with the right sort of chap
Well look where I am now, on a desert island
With so far as I can see no one at all on hand
I know what has happened though I suppose Mother wouldn't see
This hat being so strong has completely run away with me
I had the feeling it was beginning to happen the moment I put it on
What a moment that was as I rose up, I rose up like a flying swan
As strong as a swan too, why see how far my hat has flown me away
It took us a night to come and then a night and a day
And all the time the swan wing in my hat waved beautifully
Ah, I thought, How this hat becomes me.
First the sea was dark but then it was pale blue
And still the wing beat and we flew and we flew
A night and a day and a night, and by the old right way
Between the sun and the moon we flew until morning day.
It is always early morning here on this peculiar island
The green grass grows into the sea on the dipping land
Am I glad I am Here? Yes, well, I am,

It's nice to be rid of Father, Mother and the young man
There's just one thing causes me a twinge of pain,
If I take my hat off, shall I find myself home again?
So in this early morning land I always wear my hat
Go home, you see, well I wouldn't run a risk like that.

Wallace Stevens

THE EMPEROR OF ICE-CREAM

Call the roller of big cigars,
The muscular one, and bid him whip
In kitchen cups concupiscent curds.
Let the wenches dawdle in such dress
As they are used to wear, and let the boys
Bring flowers in last month's newspapers.
Let be be finale of seem.
The only emperor is the emperor of ice-cream.

Take from the dresser of deal
Lacking the three glass knobs, that sheet
On which she embroidered fantails once
And spread it so as to cover her face.
If her horny feet protrude, they come
To show how cold she is, and dumb.
Let the lamp affix its beam.
The only emperor is the emperor of ice-cream.

Anonymous

WHAT A WONDERFUL BIRD

What a wonderful bird the frog are!
When he stand he sit almost;
When he hop he fly almost.
He ain't got no sense hardly;
He ain't got no tail hardly either.
When he sit, he sit on what he ain't got almost.

Matthew Sweeney

THE FLYING SPRING ONION

The flying spring onion
flew through the air
over to where
the tomatoes grew in rows
and he said to those
seed-filled creatures
My rooted days are done,
so while you sit here
sucking sun
I'll be away and gone,
to Greenland
where they eat no green
and I won't be seen
in a salad bowl with you,
stung by lemon,
greased by oil,
and nothing at all to do
except wait to be eaten.
With that he twirled
his green propellers
and rose above the rows
of red balls
who stared as he grew small
and disappeared.

THE MONEY TREE

Listen, there *is* a money tree.
I know you don't believe me,
and I didn't when Bill told me
that his mate Joe's brother
waters it every day.

It's not just water – there's sweat
and blood mixed in, not so's
you'd notice, Joe's brother says,
and he should know because
he mixes it himself.

There's another works with him,
another money-gardener
and they hate each other,
watch each other like dogs –
that's part of the job.

The tree is in a courtyard
surrounded by blank walls
with slits for rifles,
and a ceiling of perspex
that can slide open.

Where is the courtyard?
Joe's brother doesn't know.
Every morning he has to go
to a rooftop in the city
where a copter lands.

They put on a blindfold
and no-one speaks. They whirr
Joe's brother somewhere
in the city, he can't say.
It's best he can't.

Why is there only one tree?
That's what I want to know.
You'd think they'd grow
plantations of the stuff.
Joe's brother laughs.

BIG ROCK CANDY MOUNTAINS

One evening as the sun went down and the jungle fire was
    burning
Down the track came a hobo hiking and he said boys I'm not
    turning
I'm headin for a land that's far away beside the crystal fountains
So come with me we'll go and see the Big Rock Candy
    Mountains

In the Big Rock Candy Mountains there's a land that's fair and
    bright
Where the handouts grow on bushes and you sleep out every
    night
Where the boxcars are all empty and the sun shines every day
On the birds and the bees and the cigarette trees
Where the lemonade springs where the bluebird sings
In the Big Rock Candy Mountains

In the Big Rock Candy Mountains all the cops have wooden
    legs
And the bulldogs all have rubber teeth and the hens lay soft
    boiled eggs
The farmer's trees are full of fruit and the barns are full of hay
Oh, I'm bound to go where there ain't no snow
Where the rain don't fall and the wind don't blow
In the Big Rock Candy Mountains

American Folk Rhyme

In the Big Rock Candy Mountains you never change your socks
And the little streams of alcohol come a-trickling down the rocks
The brakemen have to tip their hats and the railroad bulls are blind
There's a lake of stew and of whiskey too
You can paddle all around 'em in a big canoe
In the Big Rock Candy Mountains

In the Big Rock Candy Mountains the jails are made of tin
And you can walk right out again as soon as you are in
There ain't no short handled shovels, no axes saws or picks
I'm a going to stay where you sleep all day
Where they hung the jerk that invented work
In the Big Rock Candy Mountains
I'll see you all this coming fall in the Big Rock Candy Mountains

Anonymous

THE COMMON CORMORANT

The common cormorant or shag
Lays eggs inside a paper bag
The reason you will see no doubt –
It is to keep the lightning out.
But what these unobservant birds
Have never noticed is that herds
Of wandering bears may come with buns
And steal the bags to hold the crumbs.

Jonathan Swift

I WALK BEFORE NO MAN
(composed while asleep)

I walk before no man, a hawk in his fist;
Nor am I brilliant, whenever I list.

Anonymous

'TIS MIDNIGHT

'Tis midnight, and the setting sun
    Is slowly rising in the west;
The rapid rivers slowly run,
    The frog is on his downy nest.
The pensive goat and sportive cow
    Hilarious, leap from bough to bough.

245

ACKNOWLEDGEMENTS

Editor's acknowledgements:
I am particularly grateful to Luke Guinness for his expertise on Edward Gorey and to Jonathan Guinness for some excellent suggestions. I would also like to thank Katy Moran and Clémence Jacquinet for all their steady help with this book.

Everyman's Library gratefully acknowledges permission to reprint copyright material as follows:

HILAIRE BELLOC: 'The Frog' by Hilaire Belloc reprinted by kind permission of PFD on behalf of the Estate of Hilaire Belloc © The Estate of Hilaire Belloc 1930.
ELIZABETH BISHOP: 'The Man-Moth' from *The Complete Poems: 1927–1979* by Elizabeth Bishop. Copyright © 1979, 1983 by Alice Helen Methfessel. Reprinted by kind permission of Farrar, Straus and Giroux, LLC.
QUENTIN BLAKE: For the illustrations by Quentin Blake accompanying 'Dickery Dickery Dare' (anon.), 'I Had a Little Husband' (anon.), 'Little Blue Ben' (anon.), 'Oh, Mother, I Shall Be Married' (anon.) from *Quentin Blake's Nursery Rhyme Book* published by Jonathan Cape. Copyright © 1983 Quentin Blake. Reproduced by kind permission of The Random House Group. From *Mister Magnolia* by Quentin Blake © 1980 Quentin Blake, reprinted by kind permission of the Random House Group Ltd and A.P. Watt Ltd on behalf of Quentin Blake. 'Mustard', 'The Panda', 'The Ostrich', 'The Hippopotamus' and 'The Wombat' (illustrations) from *Custard and Company*, poems by Ogden Nash, illustrated by Quentin Blake (Puffin 1979). Text © Ogden Nash 1979. Illustrations © Quentin Blake. Reprinted by kind permission of Puffin and A.P. Watt Ltd on behalf of Quentin Blake.
G.K. CHESTERTON: 'The Oneness of the Philosopher with Nature' from *Greybeards at Play*. Text and illustration © 1964 G.K. Chesterton. Reprinted by kind permission of A.P. Watt Ltd on behalf of the Royal Literary Fund.
EMMA CHICHESTER CLARK: For the illustrations accompanying 'A Farmer Went Trotting', 'Be Lenient With Lobsters' (anon.), 'Calico Pie' (anon.), 'The Common Cormorant' (anon.) 'The Elephant is a Graceful Bird' (anon.), 'Our Yak' and 'What a Wonderful Bird' (anon.); 'The Frog' by Hilaire Belloc, 'Purple Cow' by Gelett Burgess, 'The Crocodile', 'There was a Pig', 'Twinkle Twinkle Little Bat' by Lewis Carroll, 'The Owl and the Pussy-cat', 'The Quangle Wangle's Hat' and 'There was an

Old Man' by Edward Lear, from *I Never Saw a Purple Cow*, selected and illustrated by Emma Chichester Clark. Illustrations © 1990 Emma Chichester Clark. Reproduced by kind permission of Walker Books, London SE11 5HJ. Jacket illustration © 2004 Emma Chichester Clark.

WALTER DE LA MARE: 'Kiph' by Walter de la Mare from *The Complete Poems of Walter de la Mare*, 1969 (USA: 1970). Reproduced by kind permission of the Literary Trustees of Walter de la Mare and the Society of Authors as their representative.

WILLIAM EMPSON: 'Mother, saying Anne good night' from *The Royal Beasts and Other Works* by William Empson published by Chatto & Windus. Reproduced by kind permission of Curtis Brown Ltd, London, on behalf of the William Empson Estate © William Empson.

JAMES FENTON: 'This Octopus Exploits Women' by James Fenton from *The Memory of War and Children in Exile: Poems 1968 – 1983* published by Penguin © James Fenton 1983. Reprinted by kind permission of PFD on behalf of James Fenton.

EDWARD GOREY: 'The Untitled Book' and 'The Osbick Bird' from *Amphigorey Too* © 1975 Edward Gorey and 'The Utter Zoo Alphabet' from *Amphigorey Also* © 1983 Edward Gorey. Reproduced by kind permission of the Estate of Edward Gorey.

HARRY GRAHAM: 'The Fond Father', 'The Perils of Obesity', 'Grandpapa', 'Patience' from *Ruthless Rhymes*, collection © 1984 Harry Graham. Reprinted by kind permission of the Estate of Virginia Thesiger.

TED HUGHES: 'Wodwo' from *Selected Poems: 1957–1994* by Ted Hughes. Copyright © 2002 by The Estate of Ted Hughes. Reprinted by kind permission of Farrar, Straus and Giroux, LLC and Faber & Faber.

ROGER MCGOUGH: 'Kung Fu Lee', 'Uncle Bram', 'Wild Sitting Bull', 'Cousin Fosbury', 'Eno', 'Elmer Hoover' from *Sporting Relations* by Roger McGough (copyright © Roger McGough 1996) are reproduced by kind permission of PFD (www.pfd.co.uk) on behalf of Roger McGough.

SPIKE MILLIGAN: 'A Thousand Hairy Savages', 'Hipporhinostricow', 'Can a Parrot', 'On the Ning Nang Nong', 'The Land of the Bumbley Boo', 'Maveric', 'The Bongaloo', 'The Twit' reprinted by kind permission of Spike Milligan Productions Ltd.

A.A. MILNE: 'Cottleston Pie'. From *Winnie the Pooh* by A.A. Milne. Copyright under the Berne Convention. Published by Egmont Books Limited, London and used with permission, and from *Winne-The-Pooh* by A.A. Milne © 1926 by E.P. Dutton, renewed 1954 by A.A. Milne, used by permission of Dutton children's books, a division of Penguin Young Reader's Group, a member of Penguin Group (USA) Inc, 345 Hudson St, New York, NY 10014. All rights reserved.

Acknowledgements

OGDEN NASH: For 'The Grackle', 'The Wombat', 'The Panda', 'The Ostrich' and 'The Hippopotamus' from *Candy is Dandy* (André Deutsch, 1994) reproduced by kind permission of the Carlton Publishing Group. The same poems, along with 'Mustard', are reproduced by kind permission of Curtis Brown Ltd. 'The Grackle' copyright © 1966 in *McCall's Magazine*, 'The Wombat' copyright © 1933 in the *Saturday Evening Post*, 'The Panda' copyright © 1942 in *The New Yorker*, 'The Ostrich' copyright © 1956 in *The New Yorker*, 'The Hippopotamus' copyright © 1935 in the *Saturday Evening Post*, 'Mustard' copyright © 1957 in *House and Garden*.

MERVYN PEAKE: For *The Hunting of the Snark, An Agony in Eight Fits* by Lewis Carroll, illustrated by Mervyn Peake and published by Methuen Publishing Limited, London (2000). Illustrations copyright © The Estate of Mervyn Peake 2000. For 'O'er Seas That Have No Beaches', 'Crown Me with Hairpins', 'Of Pygmies, Palms and Pirates', 'I Cannot Give the Reasons', and 'Come Break The News To Me Sweet Horse' from *A Book of Nonsense* © 1976 by Mervyn Peake. Reproduced by kind permission of Peter Owen Ltd, London.

THEODORE ROETHKE: For 'Mips and Ma' from from 'Praise to the End!' © 1950 by Theodore Roethke, from *Collected Poems of Theodore Roethke* by Theodore Roethke. Used by permission of Doubleday, a division of Random House, Inc and Faber & Faber.

STEVIE SMITH: For 'My Hat' by Stevie Smith, from *Collected Poems of Stevie Smith*, copyright © 1972 by Stevie Smith. Reprinted by kind permission of the Estate of James MacGibbon and New Directions Publishing Corp. SALES TERRITORY: U.S., Canadian and open market rights only.

WALLACE STEVENS: For 'The Emperor of Ice-cream' by Wallace Stevens from *The Collected Poems of Wallace Stevens* by Wallace Stevens © 1954 by Wallace Stevens and renewed 1982 by Holly Stevens. Used by permission of Alfred A. Knopf, a division of Random House, Inc and Faber & Faber.

MATTHEW SWEENEY: For 'The Flying Spring Onion', and 'The Money Tree' from *The Flying Spring Onion* © 1992 by Matthew Sweeney, reprinted by kind permission of Faber & Faber.

TOMI UNGERER: For illustrations accompanying 'The Boy Stood on the Burning Deck' (anon.) and 'The King Said to Salome' (anon.) from *Oh, How Silly!* published by Methuen © 1970 by Tomi Ungerer, reprinted by kind permission of Diogenes Publishing.

INDEX OF POEMS AND FIRST LINES

Index of poems and first lines

LIST OF ILLUSTRATIONS

List of illustrations

256